FOR HIS
DAUGHTER'S
SAKE

FOR HIS DAUGHTER'S SAKE

STELLA BAGWELL

MILLS & BOON

First published in Great Britain 2021
by Mills & Boon, an imprint of HarperCollins*Publishers* Ltd,
1 London Bridge Street, London, SE1 9GF

www.harpercollins.co.uk

HarperCollins*Publishers*
1st Floor, Watermarque Building,
Ringsend Road, Dublin 4, Ireland

Large Print edition 2021

For His Daughter's Sake © 2021 Harlequin Books S.A.

Special thanks and acknowledgement are given to
Stella Bagwell for her contribution to the
Montana Mavericks: The Real Cowboys of Bronco

ISBN: 978-0-263-29023-3

08/21

MIX
Paper from
responsible sources
FSC™ C007454

Printed and bound in Great Britain
by CPI Group (UK) Ltd, Croydon, CR0 4YY

To my late mother, Lucille.
Even though you were born
a hundred years ago, your warm love
still lives on in my heart.

Chapter One

Callie Sheldrick carefully hid a bored yawn behind her hand as she watched Melanie Driscoll, the honoree of tonight's bridal shower, open one of the many gift-wrapped boxes stacked on a decorated table.

"An air fryer! I can't wait to try this!" Melanie exclaimed. "When Gabe asks for fried food, I won't have to remind him about the fat and extra calories!"

Several of the women seated in a semicircle around the table where the pretty blonde was busily tearing into another gift began talking at once, extolling the virtues of the air fryer. Until the next gift emerged and more squeals of delight and claps of approval rippled through the shower guests.

"A blender!" Angela, the mother of the groom, chimed out. "How perfect! Now you can make all kinds of smoothies for you and Gabe!"

Callie rolled her eyes toward the ceiling and wondered if there was something wrong with her. Why were these women getting so excited over kitchen gadgets that would probably end up doing little more than collecting dust?

In all fairness, Callie might get excited about kitchen appliances if she knew how to cook. But she was totally lost when it came to preparing food, and the fact didn't bother her in the least. Besides, she wasn't the one getting married, she thought glumly. No, she was one of the few women left in Bronco, Montana, who wasn't wearing an engagement ring or, for that matter, even dating anyone.

"That's the second time you've yawned in

the past five minutes," Vanessa Cruise said in a low voice next to Callie's ear. "Didn't you get enough sleep last night?"

Callie glanced at her friend and roommate. Vanessa would probably be the next to have a wedding shower. The pretty brunette wasn't engaged with a ring yet, but she suspected Vanessa's boyfriend, Jameson John, would most likely surprise her with a sparkler any day now.

Stifling a sigh, Callie tried not to think that sooner, rather than later, Vanessa would be Jameson's wife and living on his ranch. Callie didn't want to dwell on the thought of her roommate moving out of the apartment. And she definitely didn't want to think about how her own boyfriend had ended their relationship and skipped town right before Christmas. Now that it was August and months had slipped by, she'd gotten over the sting of Zach's rejection. But that hardly meant she wasn't lonely.

She was, in fact, very lonely.

"Oh, I thought I had hidden the yawns

behind my hand. Sorry. I hope no one else noticed. Especially Mel. This is her special night. And it is a beautiful shower." Callie gestured around the elaborately furnished den on the Ambling A. "This house isn't a ranch house. From what I've seen, it's more like a modern-day castle with a Western flair. And this room has been turned into a fairyland with all the decorations. The flowers alone must have cost a fortune."

"It's all gorgeous," Vanessa agreed. "The pink and coral color scheme is dreamy. I'm betting those are the colors Mel has chosen to use at her wedding."

"With the wedding at the end of the month, she must be going crazy with all the planning right now. Especially when it will be a fairy-tale event."

"Anything less wouldn't be fitting for an Abernathy," Vanessa told her. "And then we'll have Jordan Taylor and Camilla Sanchez's wedding to look forward to."

Callie's sigh was wistful. "It's really incredible how many couples here in Bronco have paired off this past year."

Two middle-aged women sitting a short distance from Callie and Vanessa must've heard them discussing engagements and weddings. Both glanced in Callie's direction before exchanging conspiratorial smiles.

"It's good that Gabe is getting married, but it's high time someone finds a nice girl for his cousin, Tyler Abernathy," one of the women said.

"Why, you can take one look at the man and see that he needs a good woman in his life," the second woman replied.

Callie avoided glancing at the talkative pair, even though she was shocked by their comments.

Back in July, at the Bronco Barbecue during the Fourth of July celebration, Callie had taken notice of Tyler Abernathy. He'd been helping his four brothers run the booth for Abernathy Meats. Tall, with very dark hair and a somber expression, he had a quality that had caught Callie's attention. But then she'd dared to take a second glance and that's when she'd noticed he was carrying a baby in a BabyBjörn, and wearing a wedding band on his left hand. Now these women were saying he needed a wife? It was scandalous!

Confused, Callie glanced over at Vanessa to ask whether she knew the details of Tyler's marital status, but her roommate was caught up in a conversation with Cassidy Ware, the perky young blonde who owned Bronco Java and Juice in downtown Bronco Heights.

"Such a sad situation." One of the women across the way spoke again. "Losing his wife in a car accident when little Maeve was only three months old. I don't know how the young man has been able to hold himself together."

"I'll tell you how," a third woman sitting beside them interjected. "The Abernathys are strong stock. The family won't allow Tyler to fall apart. He has those four strapping brothers to help him out."

"Yes, but brothers can't replace a wife,"

one said. "And if you ask me, Tyler's quite a catch."

A few of the women who'd jumped into the conversation agreed with the idea of Tyler being a catch. But two of the older women near them shook their heads.

"I can't see it. Changing diapers and walking the floor with a crying baby. That's no way for a new wife to start a marriage."

"Right," the other agreed. "She'd end up being a glorified babysitter. Not a real wife. And Tyler's only been a widower for six months. The last thing on his mind is finding a new love."

Callie tried to ignore the gossiping voices as her mind whirled with the fact that Tyler was a widower. How terrible for him and for his daughter. The little girl would never know her biological mother.

Oh Lord, Callie should be ashamed for ever being attracted to the man in the first place. But she'd truly not known about the tragic situation.

Needing a moment to compose herself,

she leaned her head toward Vanessa's. "I'm going to the powder room."

Her friend frowned. "Are you okay? You look pale."

In spite of feeling a bit shaken, she said, "I'm fine. I'll be right back."

With Melanie continuing to open the stack of festively wrapped gifts, no one noticed Callie's slipping away. At least, she didn't think anyone had noticed. But as soon as she left the powder room to return to the den, ninety-four-year-old Winona Cobbs, the town's psychic, waylaid her.

This evening the woman was dressed in her usual flamboyant style. A red-and-white-striped jumpsuit with billowy legs and sleeves swallowed her tiny figure, while a headband covered with red silk flowers held her long white hair back from her face.

She said, "Let's go sit a minute, Callie."

Callie was trying to think of a polite excuse to hurry back to the party, but words failed her as Winona's frail hand grabbed her by the forearm and led her over to a pair of chairs near the refreshment table.

Since Winona's consulting business had moved inside the Bronco Ghost Tours offices where Callie worked as administrative assistant to Evan Cruise, she saw the old woman coming and going every day. But Winona had never done anything more than say hello or lift a hand in greeting. Why had she chosen tonight to corner Callie?

"I really hate to miss seeing Melanie open the last of her gifts," Callie said politely. "Did you have something important to tell me? Something about Evan?"

With a vague smile on her wrinkled face, Winona patted the back of Callie's hand. "This isn't about my great-grandson. This is about you, Callie. You need to be aware that the time has come."

Really? For what? The refreshments to be served? Callie tried not to look any more bored than she had when Melanie had pulled out the air fryer. "I don't understand. The time has come for what?"

Winona gave her a knowing nod. "When it happens, you'll understand. The signal is strong. I can feel it."

Callie found it hard to believe that people actually consulted Winona for psychic readings. They could probably make just as much sense from a fortune cookie, she thought.

Smiling wanly, she decided the only thing to do was to placate the old woman. "I wish I could feel *it* like you're feeling *it*."

Winona's eyes were sparkling, as though she were eyeing a pot of gold. "You will, Callie. You're not feeling the signal now because you're fighting it. But don't be afraid."

Why should she be afraid? Was the signal coming from an alien planet? she wanted to ask Winona. "Afraid of what?" Callie had to query.

Confident she'd gotten the message across, Winona rose. "Everything will be clear—in time."

With those parting words, Winona went on her way. Callie stared after her for a moment, then, with a confused shake of her head, hurriedly returned to her seat next to Vanessa.

"Have you been in the powder room all this time?" her friend asked. "I was about to come looking for you."

Callie whispered under her breath, "I was on my way back when your great-grandmother waylaid me. I couldn't get away from her. Not without seeming rude."

Vanessa arched a brow at her. "Winona? What did she want with you?"

"If I ever figure it out, I'll let you know," Callie said wryly, then inclined her head toward Melanie, who was still ripping open gifts. "What did I miss? More kitchen appliances?"

"A toaster oven, a steam iron and a set of cast-aluminum cookware."

Callie tried not to grimace. "Sounds like Mel will be able to spend days in the kitchen and never have to come out."

Vanessa frowned at her. "Why, Callie, where is that sarcasm coming from? Aren't you happy for Mel and Gabe?"

"Of course, I'm happy for them," Callie said, hating herself for sounding so childish. "And I'm sorry if I sound petulant. To be honest, I'm feeling a bit left out. All of you have someone, Van. A man standing proudly at your side—loving you and planning a future with you. I suppose I'm wondering if I'll ever find my once-in-a-lifetime love, or if I'm destined to always be alone."

"Don't be ridiculous. Mr. Right is going to come along for you, and soon. I just have a feeling."

Callie rolled her brown eyes. "You're beginning to sound more like your great-grandmother every day."

Vanessa laughed. "Maybe mystic powers run in the family."

Attending his cousin's party tonight at DJ's Deluxe was the last thing Tyler Abernathy had wanted to do.

Already exhausted from herding calves to the branding chute all morning, not to mention seeing after his baby daughter for the remainder of the day, he hadn't felt like driving into Bronco to meet his brothers and friends at the fancy barbecue place. But his cousin Gabe was getting married at the end of the month and, while Melanie was enjoying a bridal shower, Gabe was having his own little celebration with the guys. And Tyler could hardly blame him. It wasn't every day that a man married the woman of his dreams.

To make this day even worse, since Tyler's mother and all his female cousins were attending the bridal shower at the Ambling A this evening, there'd been no one to babysit Maeve. Not that taking his daughter with him was anything unusual. Since Luanne's death six months ago, he'd taken Maeve with him practically everywhere. Having her with him at the party was really nothing new. And, so far, his daughter had been a good baby.

Having decided a change of venue was in order, the group of men had exited DJ's Deluxe and headed out to the Ambling A. Tyler had considered saying his goodbyes and driving on home to the Flying A, the ranch owned and operated by his parents and their five sons, but he'd not wanted to look like a party-pooper.

Now as Tyler entered the den of the Ambling A, carrying his nine-month-old daughter in the crook of his left arm, he glanced around the room crammed full of women. Obviously, he was the first guy from the party at DJ's to arrive and he felt like a fish out of water.

He was scanning the room, trying to locate an inconspicuous place for him and Maeve to park for a few minutes, when he noticed a young brunette looking straight at him. However, as soon as Tyler turned his gaze directly on her, she shyly glanced away.

She looked vaguely familiar, but if he'd met her before, he didn't recall it. That was hardly a surprise. These past months had been a blurred nightmare for Tyler. Faces, names, even time, didn't really register with him.

"Hey, Tyler!"

He looked in the direction of the voice calling out his name and spotted his cousin motioning him to join her in a corner of the room away from the refreshment table, where many of the women were helping themselves to cake and punch.

After working his way through the female crowd, Tyler sank into a padded folding chair next to his cousin, then let out a weary sigh as he carefully set Maeve on the floor next to her baby daughter, Josie.

"Hi, Tyler. How's it going?" Erica asked.

"I'm okay. And you?"

She regarded him with a keen eye. "I'm doing great. But I'm guessing it would be safe to say you've had a long day."

His pretty blond cousin had married Morgan Dalton, a local rancher, back in November and, a few weeks later, she'd given birth to Josie. The little girl was the same age as his Maeve and both were similar in size. But there was a huge difference in the two babies. Josie was usually happy and laughing. Maeve's personality was totally unpredictable. She might be giggling one moment and crying angrily the next.

"It feels like this day has gone on forever," Tyler said. "I just left Gabe's party at DJ's Deluxe."

With a look of concern, his cousin studied him closely. "And you took Maeve with you? That couldn't have been much of a party for you."

"No matter," he said. "I only went for Gabe's sake. Not for fun."

Erica grimaced. "I don't suppose you do much of anything for fun. You know, Tyler, you really do need help with Maeve."

He handed Maeve a small stuffed animal from the diaper bag he'd carried in with him. The baby let out a happy coo and drew the little black-and-white kitty straight to her mouth.

"Maeve is my responsibility, Erica. I promised Luanne I'd take care of her, and I can't let her down."

"Luanne is gone, Tyler," Erica said gently. "But I imagine if she could see you now, wearing yourself razor-thin, she wouldn't be happy."

Erica was right. His late wife wouldn't be happy, Tyler thought ruefully. While Luanne had been alive, she'd been angry with him during most of their marriage. He'd never been able to make her happy.

"Mom and all my cousins, including you, are here at the shower. I didn't have anyone to babysit."

"You could've dropped Maeve off at a childcare center in town before you went to DJ's," Erica suggested. "I think there's one that has late hours."

Tyler scowled at her. "While I watched the guys eat barbecue and down beers? That wasn't going to happen."

He'd barely gotten the remark out when the sound of male voices entering the den caught everyone's attention. Glancing over his right shoulder, he watched his brothers and Gabe laugh and banter their way to a table displaying unwrapped gifts.

"Looks like that bunch is feeling good.

Maybe you should've had a few rounds with them. At least it might have put a smile on your face," Erica suggested.

"No alcohol for me. I have enough trouble staying awake as it is." Swinging his gaze back to his daughter, he noticed her crawling away. He quickly sat her back at his feet and fetched a teething ring from the diaper bag. She took the bright red rubber ring, but he doubted it would keep her pacified for very long.

Not caring that the party was far from over, or what anyone would think of his leaving early, Tyler decided he would give Melanie and Gabe his best wishes and then take his daughter home.

As that resolving thought formed in his head, he glanced over to his left and saw her—the brunette—again. Even though she was standing with her back to Tyler, he recognized the brown wavy hair and petite figure dressed in a summery pink dress that floated around her knees.

"Who's the woman with Vanessa Cruise?

She looks familiar, but I can't place her," Tyler said to Erica.

His cousin glanced in the direction of the two women. "That's Callie Sheldrick. And you ought to recognize her. She's Evan's administrative assistant for Bronco Ghost Tours. I'll call her over."

"Uh—no, that's okay. Don't bother her," Tyler said quickly, wishing he'd kept his mouth shut.

Ignoring his protest, Erica quickly motioned for the woman's attention. "Callie! Over here!"

As the young woman made her way across, Tyler rose politely.

"I called you over because I thought you might want to meet one of Gabe's cousins," Erica told Callie. "He thinks he might've met you before."

Tyler watched a pair of big brown eyes turn in his direction and, as her gaze settled on his face, felt a most unusual punch to his gut.

"Oh, you probably saw me last month at the Fourth of July barbecue. You and your brothers were running a booth—selling Abernathy meats."

Tyler quickly searched his memory, but for the life of him, couldn't recall seeing this pretty brunette that day. But it wasn't like him to take a second glance at any woman. In fact, he'd only noticed this one tonight because she'd been openly staring at him. Until she'd realized he'd spotted her, and then she'd looked away as though she'd been caught with her hand in the cookie jar.

"I, uh…maybe that's where I saw you," he said finally, frowning. "Did we talk? Uh, to each other, I mean?"

Red color was seeping into her cheeks and Tyler could see that she was embarrassed for some reason. Because it was obvious he couldn't remember meeting her? Or because she hadn't forgotten seeing him?

"No," she replied. "You and your brothers were very busy that day. I was there at your booth with a friend. That's all. No big deal."

Seeing Maeve was about to crawl off again, he picked her up and settled her in the crook of one arm before he thrust a hand out to the woman. "Well, I'm Tyler Abernathy and this little mover and shaker is my daughter, Maeve."

The brunette barely touched her hand to his and Tyler wondered if she was always this shy or if something about him was putting her off.

"Nice to meet you," she murmured. "I'm Callie Sheldrick."

She turned her gaze on Maeve and, as if on cue, his daughter burst out crying.

The woman took a step back, as though her presence had brought on Maeve's loud cries. "Oh, I'm sorry. I didn't mean to disturb the baby."

Frowning, Tyler automatically bounced Maeve up and down in an effort to quiet her, while Callie continued to back farther away.

"Maeve's crying has nothing to do with you, Callie."

"Sorry," she said and then, with a shake of her head, turned and hurried away.

Totally confused, Tyler glanced at Erica.

Because Maeve had started to cry, Josie had become upset and crawled into her mother's lap and was whimpering for attention. Great, he thought. As usual, his ineptness at fatherhood was causing a mess all around.

"What was that all about?" Tyler asked. "She looked like she thought Maeve was going to morph into a little monster."

Erica batted one hand through the air. "Callie isn't that experienced with babies. Little ones like ours make some people nervous. Why don't you take Maeve over and get her some cake or punch?"

"And put her on a sugar high? I'll never get her to sleep tonight."

Laughing, Erica shook her head. "Tyler, you desperately need to lighten up on yourself and Maeve. A few sips of punch or a bite of cake isn't going to send your daughter on a rampage. This is a party. Let her enjoy it."

Lighten up. Enjoy. Have fun. These past few months, he'd heard those very same words from his parents and brothers. Deep down, he understood they were well-mean-ing and even right. But how was he supposed to feel joy while his mind and heart were riddled with guilt?

The time has come. Ever since Winona had sat her down and plied her with prophetic quips, Callie had wondered what they could possibly mean. Now, after meeting Tyler Abernathy, she'd figured out one of them. The time had come for her to make a big fool of herself.

Callie had always been on the shy side, but not enough to make her sound tongue-tied or loopy. Yet the moment she'd looked into Tyler's blue eyes, something had gone haywire. Not one coherent thought had been able to form in her head. And then when his baby had taken one look at her and burst into tears, she'd felt so embarrassed she'd wanted to run and hide.

That had been ten minutes ago and she'd come to the conclusion that she wasn't going to see this party to the end. Callie had driven Vanessa out here to the ranch, but she figured her roommate wouldn't have any trouble catching a ride back into town with some of their other friends.

With that thought in mind, Callie stood on tiptoes and began searching the crowd for Vanessa.

"Lost something?"

The question came in the form of a male voice that sounded vaguely familiar. Callie's heart thumped wildly as she slowly turned to see Tyler standing directly behind her. A faint smile was on his face, while the baby girl in his arms looked at Callie and let out a happy shriek.

Don't make a fool of yourself again, Callie. Just keep your cool and don't let him guess that something about him makes your pulse skyrocket.

"Not exactly. I was looking for my roommate," she told him. "To tell her I was thinking of going home."

"Oh. Looks like things here are still going strong," he said. "You might miss something."

Like seeing Melanie open more kitchen appliances or fancy linens to go on the bride and groom's bed, Callie thought wryly. For some reason she couldn't quite explain, the thought made her feel even more lonely and sad.

"Believe me, Mel will never miss me."

He smiled and Callie could feel her heart make a weird lurch beneath her breast.

"She or Gabe wouldn't miss me, either. But Erica insists I need to stay and enjoy myself."

"Are you? Uh, going to stay longer?" she asked.

He shrugged. "Only for a few more minutes. I wanted to find you—to apologize for Maeve upsetting you with her crying."

"Oh no. I should be apologizing to you for making her cry. Until I walked up, she appeared perfectly happy."

He grunted with amusement. "Believe me, you didn't cause all that bawling. She does that quite often and I never know what triggers it."

"Really? I thought it was me. I'm glad it wasn't."

He smiled again and the expression made his features even more handsome.

"See, neither one of us has anything to apologize for," he said.

She smiled back at him then glanced tentatively at the baby. The little girl was truly adorable with the few light brownish-blond curls covering the top of her head and wisps around her angelic face. Her blue eyes were like her father's. So were the dimples denting both cheeks. But other than that, Callie didn't see a lot of resemblance between the two.

"I guess not," she said to him. Spotting Vanessa across the room, she added, "I see my friend. I'd better go catch up with her. Nice talking with you, Tyler."

He inclined his head toward her. "Good night, Callie. Be sure and drive home safely."

"Of course."

As he turned and disappeared into the crowd, it dawned on Callie that his advice must have stemmed from the loss of his wife. Obviously, he was still grieving for the woman he'd loved, she thought sadly. And any woman who attempted to step into Tyler Abernathy's life at this point would end up competing with a ghost.

One more reason Callie needed to forget the sexy rancher.

Chapter Two

Standing at the side of his daughter's crib, Tyler tucked a light blanket around her shoulders. Then, after placing a kiss on her cheek, he stood gazing down at her sweet face. As soon as they'd left the party and started home, Maeve had fallen asleep in her car carrier. Even after he'd carried her into the house and changed her little dress for a pink onesie, she hadn't stirred.

No doubt she was tired from the long and busy day that had started early this morning with a trip to his parents' house where his mother, Hannah, had watched Maeve for a few hours while Tyler had helped his brothers with the branding. Later, he'd picked up his daughter and the two of them had driven out to another part of the Flying A to check on a herd of newly weaned calves.

By the time they'd returned home and he'd gotten Maeve dressed and ready for Gabe's party, she'd been cranky and needing a nap. The drive into Bronco had given her a few minutes of sleep and, wonder of wonders, had been enough to improve her mood. She'd been fairly jolly until Callie Sheldrick had walked up.

Releasing a heavy breath, he turned away from the crib and, after switching on a night-light, walked out to the den, where he slumped tiredly into a leather armchair and propped his feet on a matching footstool.

At this late hour, he should be in bed. Tomorrow was going to be another busy day helping his father rake and bale the last of the hay meadow. Tyler didn't want to start out the day dog-tired. But he knew it would be useless to crawl into bed right now. No matter how hard he tried, he couldn't seem to calm his tumbling thoughts. Or quit thinking about Callie Sheldrick.

What was going on with him anyway? Since Luanne's death, he couldn't think of one time he'd taken a second look at any woman. He'd lost all desire for female company and, frankly, he'd been glad about that malady. His life was already complicated enough without adding a woman in the mix.

For the past six months, he'd been consumed with learning how to be a full-time father to Maeve. And although he was getting better at dealing with the baby, he could admit there were times he was clueless about how to cope with crying jags, tummy aches, teething and the need for constant attention.

His brain was already bogged down with too many memories of dead dreams and tons of guilt. Why weigh it even more with thoughts of Callie? She was hardly a glamour girl, or even a head-turning beauty, he mentally argued. Even so, she was pretty, with her soft, sweet features and skin so smooth it appeared poreless. And those big brown eyes... He'd seen something warm and inviting in their dark depths. Something that had touched him in a most unexpected way.

Damn it. If he was a drinking man... He could slug down a shot or two of bourbon and wait for the alcohol to clear his wandering thoughts. But Tyler wasn't a drinker. And that was a good thing. Otherwise, he would've probably already turned into an alcoholic.

Pushing himself from the chair, he walked out to the kitchen, filled a small saucepan with milk and then placed it on the gas range to heat. While he waited, he removed his cell phone from the pocket of his Western shirt and set it on the kitchen table before opening the pearl snaps and slipping the garment off his shoulders.

Once he'd tossed it onto a chair at the table, he took a bottle of chocolate syrup from the cupboard. Squirting the syrup into the milk until it turned brown, he then added a big spoonful of sugar. The drink wouldn't taste as good as the hot chocolate his mother made on cold, snowy nights, but it would be better than nothing.

Before he'd married Luanne, Tyler hadn't known anything about cooking. He'd grown up learning about raising cattle, riding horses, and all the things it took to keep a ranch going and profitable. Now that he was on his own, though, he was learning how to fend for himself, even if most of the time he resorted to ready-made meals heated in the microwave. As for Maeve, formula and baby food made the task of feeding his daughter a bit simpler.

With the hot chocolate poured into a mug, he sat at the kitchen table and took a few cautious sips. Maybe by the time he reached the bottom of the mug, he'd quit all this thinking and remembering. He could only hope.

The ring of the cell phone interrupted his thoughts and he quickly glanced at the screen to see who was calling. Barring an emergency, he couldn't think of anyone who might be calling at this late hour.

Spotting his brother's name, he snatched up the phone and swiped it to answer.

"Dean? What's wrong?"

His brother chuckled. "Calm down, Ty. Nothing is wrong. I was just checking to make sure you and Maeve made it home okay."

"Oh." He let out a long breath of relief. "Sure. Maeve is already sound asleep in her crib and I'm having a cup of hot chocolate."

Dean chuckled again. "Hot chocolate when beer was flowing at DJ's?"

"I didn't touch any beer. Not when I'd be driving with Maeve," he said flatly.

There was an awkward pause and then Dean said, "Sorry. I wasn't thinking about Maeve. Guess that shows you how little I know about having a baby around. I don't envy you, Ty, but I admire you for being such a diligent father to my little niece."

As always, when someone praised him for being a good father, guilt swamped him. For a moment, it was all Tyler could do not to curse at his older brother, to tell him he didn't know what the hell he was talking about, but somehow he managed to bite back the words. Dean didn't deserve to have Tyler's bitterness spewed at him.

Wiping a hand over his face, he said, "It didn't hurt me to give up a few beers, Dean."

"No. I suppose not. But sometimes I wish…"

Tyler drank the last of the warm, chocolaty milk. "What? That your baby brother would loosen up? Well, I've already heard that once tonight. You might as well say it, too."

"Who told you that? The little brunette I saw you talking to at the shower?"

Tyler was momentarily stunned by his brother's question. He'd only exchanged a few words with Callie and yet Dean made it sound like the two of them had been cloistered in a corner, making flirty eyes at each other. Yeah, as if he'd remember how to do that, he thought dourly.

"For your information, Erica was the one who kindly told me to lighten up on myself. The 'little brunette,' as you call her, was only saying hello. She happens to be Evan Cruise's administrative assistant."

Dean said, "Oh, I didn't know. I thought you might've been talking to her about becoming Maeve's nanny. But, to tell you the truth, I was hoping you were asking her out on a date. Don't you think it's about time?"

Time. Tyler kept thinking and hoping that time would help him gather the shattered parts of his life back together. But so far, he was still a ragged mess. Tonight was the first time he'd allowed himself to think of himself as a single man, and that had only lasted for the two or three minutes he'd talked with Callie.

"You might think so, Dean. But I, uh, don't think I could handle being out with a woman—trying to think about her instead of…"

"Your dead wife," Dean said bluntly. "You might as well say it, Ty. You're not going to ever be able to move forward if you don't face up to reality."

The urge to curse at his brother hit Tyler

again but, thankfully, he found the strength to swallow the words. However, he wasn't able to keep the sarcasm from his voice as he asked, "What do you know about reality, Dean? Have you lost a wife? Do you have a child that will never know her mother?"

There was a long pause before Dean finally answered, "What has you so messed up tonight, Ty? Is it the idea of Gabe and Mel getting married? Does it remind you of everything you lost? If that's the case, you're going to have to dig down and find some inner strength from somewhere. Because we're always going to have friends or relatives falling in love and getting married. If you can't deal with that, you're going to have a mental and physical breakdown."

"I'm so glad you called tonight, brother. This is just what I needed to hear," Tyler muttered. "That I'm going to end up being a nutcase who can't take care of myself or my daughter!"

"Okay. Go ahead and wallow in self-pity,"

Dean shot back. "I'm getting sick of trying to talk sense into you. I'll talk to you later."

"Wait, Dean!" Tyler managed to bluster before his brother ended the connection. "I— You're right. I sound miserable and un-grateful. I get that you're trying to help me. I'm not myself tonight. I've had a long day and need some rest."

A few silent seconds ticked by before his older brother replied. "I understand, Ty. Up to a point. I only want you to be happy—to make an effort to be happy. No one is saying it will be easy. But I happen to have faith in you. To believe you can do better than what you're doing now."

This wasn't the first lecture or pep talk he'd gotten from a family member, and it would hardly be the last. But Tyler wasn't in the mood tonight.

"I've been trying, Dean. But it's damned hard when I'm being stretched in all direc-tions. Sometimes I feel like I'm going to snap."

Dean said, "Maybe you need to decide

what's most important to you. Showing everyone what a diligent dad you are to Maeve? Or letting them see that, like the rest of us humans, you could use a little help?"

"If you're talking about getting a full-time nanny for Maeve, forget it," he said brusquely. "She's my responsibility. I'm not going to let her down. I failed with Luanne. I can't fail with my daughter."

"The only way you can fail now, Ty, is to let the past control your future. Think about that, won't you?"

"Sure, I'll think about it." That's all he did anyway. Think until he was sure his mind was going to explode from the overload.

To Tyler's relief, Dean changed the subject and, after discussing a few projects their father had planned for the next few days, he ended the call.

Raking both hands through his hair, he went into the den and sat, resting his head against the back of the armchair.

No matter where in the house he happened to be, or even if his eyes were closed, he could still see Luanne carrying Maeve on her shoulder as she'd walked from room to room trying to calm her incessant crying.

Maeve had never been a contented baby. For the first three months of her life, she'd suffered with bouts of colic. Tyler had tried to help his wife care for their new daughter, but he'd been totally inept at quieting the baby. The moment he'd take Maeve into his arms, she would scream that much louder. He'd rocked and hummed and rubbed her tummy, anything and everything to try to soothe her. But the baby had wanted no part of him. She'd only wanted her mother.

During those first couple of months after Maeve was born, Tyler had tried to keep his unease hidden, but deep inside he'd been terrified of fatherhood. He hadn't known the first thing about baby care. Hell, he'd been a cowboy. The only kind of babies he'd ever cared for were calves and foals. Maeve had been so tiny, just holding her had nearly put him in a panic. But he'd been too embarrassed and ashamed to admit his fears to anyone.

You're only making her cry louder, Ty. She can tell you're nervous. She can feel that you don't want to hold her. You're no better at being a father than you are a husband!

Tyler figured if he lived to be a hundred he'd never forget the words Luanne had flung at him. How could he forget, when everything she'd said had been the truth? He'd been a miserable husband.

After knowing her for only a short time, he'd married a city girl from Chicago without contemplating the consequences. He'd foolishly assumed she would settle into life on the ranch and love it as much as he loved it. He hadn't considered how isolated the Montana countryside would feel to her, or how much she would miss her friends and the busy life she'd led back in the city.

Once the hot attraction that had initially pulled them together had cooled, their differences had stood like a fence between them. Luanne had begun to beg him to leave the ranch and move to Chicago where she could be near her family and the lifestyle she was accustomed to. But Tyler had refused. The ranch was his lifeblood. His home was in Montana and he'd been smart enough to know he'd be miserable trying to fit into Luanne's city life.

Arguments and silent tension had taken hold of their lives. Then Luanne had unexpectedly become pregnant and, for a while, they'd both focused on the coming child and a hope that it would draw them closer together. When Maeve had been born, they'd truly been thrilled. But then had come the hard part—caring for a tiny human being twenty-four hours a day.

For the first month, Luanne's mother had come to help her daughter with the baby. Her supportive presence had allowed Tyler to get back to his ranch duties. But once his mother-in-law had returned to Chicago, Luanne had once again been swamped with caring for a fussy baby, with no help from Tyler.

Weeks passed, but time hadn't improved the situation. Maeve had continually cried with bouts of colic and Luanne had grown ever more exhausted. Tyler's efforts had been useless and, feeling more helpless than he'd ever felt in his life, he'd begun to work later and later, doing any and every ranch chore he could find just to avoid facing Luanne's unhappiness and Maeve's crying.

Something has to give around here, Tyler. I'm exhausted! If you can't step up and be a father, then I'm going back home to Chicago and taking Maeve with me. At least there, I'll have someone who'll love and support me!

Maeve had been crying when Luanne had handed her over to Tyler and, with helpless desperation, he'd watched his wife snatch up the car keys and practically run to the front door.

I'm going out. Somewhere. Anywhere to get a break. I'll be back in a few hours.

Those had been the last words Luanne had said to him.

He had watched and waited for her return,

but she'd never made it back to the ranch. The next morning, the local authorities had found her wrecked car.

Tyler had been in shock, along with his family and the local community. Some townsfolk had even whispered and wondered why a young wife with a baby had been out driving the roads at such a late hour. After a few days, an autopsy had revealed there were no drugs or alcohol in Luanne's system. And due to the fact that it was a single-car accident with no brake marks on the highway, it was determined that she had simply fallen asleep behind the wheel.

Tyler could say exhaustion had killed her, but it wasn't that simple. As far as he was concerned, he'd killed Luanne just as surely as if he'd put her in that car and purposely pushed the vehicle off a cliff. If he'd been any kind of husband at all, he would've run after her and stopped her from driving away. He would've realized his wife had reached the breaking point. And no matter how awkward he'd felt when he'd tried to pacify Maeve's cries, he should've made a better effort to be a useful father and do his part of the parenting.

But it was too late to change the course of events that had taken Luanne's life. Even admitting he'd been a failure as a husband and father wouldn't bring her back.

Tyler's brothers and parents wanted him to move forward, to be happy. None of them really understood that Tyler was undeserving of happiness. No one realized that the only way he could make up for Luanne's death was to devote himself to caring for Maeve.

If Luanne could speak to him from the grave, she'd probably tell him his effort was too little too late. And maybe it was. But devoting himself to Maeve was all he had left.

After a second cup of coffee, Callie had sufficient energy to keep her eyelids open, although the caffeine wasn't enough to make her feel human. After a few short hours of sleep, she'd somehow managed to drag herself into work on time this morning, but only half of her brain was willing to focus on her job. The other half was stubbornly stuck on Tyler Abernathy. Darn it! She wished she'd never met him.

No. That wasn't exactly true. She'd liked meeting Tyler. She just hadn't enjoyed her stammering, red-faced reaction to the man.

Why in the world had Erica called her over in the first place? Surely the man hadn't asked to meet her, Callie thought. From the gossip she'd heard being passed around the shower guests, Tyler had only been a widower for a few short months. The thought of dating again was probably the last thing on his mind.

Yet even that sobering fact hadn't been enough to push Tyler out of Callie's thoughts. She'd spent most of the night tossing and turning while the ridiculous notion that he needed her kept running through her mind. Where was that idea coming from? Callie wasn't good with babies. She hardly knew anything about them. How could she possibly help him?

Not wanting to dwell on that question, she leaned closer to the monitor and, with a weary yawn, squinted at the list of tours scheduled for tomorrow. Saturday was always their busiest day of the week and, with tourists getting in last-minute vacations before school began next month, she expected even more traffic to pass through the doors of Bronco Ghost Tours.

"Hey, sleepyhead, want to see what I have?"

Callie looked away from the monitor to see Saundra, the spirited redhead who helped with bookings and merchandise sales.

"Let me guess. Lunch for the whole office?"

Divorced and somewhere in her midthirties, Saundra was usually in a good mood and this morning was no exception. She laughed at Callie's suggestion.

"I'm a generous person, but my wallet isn't feeling that fat right now. But I will spring for your lunch today, if you'd like to go with me to Bronco Java."

Bronco Java and Juice, a cozy coffee shop

and juice bar, also served breakfast and lunch. The food was great and the atmosphere casual. In spite of Zach never wanting to go there, it was one of Callie's favorite places to eat in Bronco Heights. But she could happily say that Zach didn't matter to her anymore. These past months she'd looked back and realized that he'd been all about himself. She didn't need or want that kind of selfish man in her life.

"That's the best offer I've had all week. I'll be ready," Callie told her, then gestured to the box. "What's really in there? A headless ghoul to hang in the window?"

Saundra chuckled again. "Not exactly, but you're close. This is Ghost Tour merchandise Evan ordered a few weeks back. It's mostly the same things we've offered for sale before, but the colors and designs are different. He wants some of it displayed in the front windows and I'm thinking we need to make some sort of spooky background to show it off better."

Frowning, Callie racked her brain to remember Evan ordering new merchandise. "My memory must've gone on the blink since then. Let's see."

Saundra carried the box over to Callie's desk and placed it on the only bare space she could find between the stacks of files and folders.

Digging into the items, Saundra pulled out two coffee mugs. "See, aren't these cute? Bronco Ghost Tours on one side and the image of a ghost on the other. Frankly, I like the red one—it goes with my hair," she said impishly. "But the black looks spookier. I'm betting the black sells out first."

Callie peered into the box. "Is that T-shirts in there, too?"

"Sure is. Not a big variety of sizes yet. Evan says he wants to see how they sell before he invests in a bunch of them. These are mainly medium and large sizes. Guess he doesn't think little things like you would want to wear one."

Callie picked up one of the shirts and held it up. Like the mugs, the garment had Bronco

Ghost Tours stamped across the chest. Below the logo was the image of several hooded, faceless ghouls wearing Stetson hats.

"Hmm. Kind of cute. These should sell. Especially when the rodeo comes to town. Or after a tour and the guests are feeling relieved that they weren't attacked by a ghost or goblin," Saundra commented.

Callie laughed. "Ridiculous, isn't it, how some people feel all creepy-crawly at the mere mention of a place being haunted?"

Saundra looked at her. "You don't?"

Shaking her head, Callie said, "I'm too practical. Or maybe a better word is *unimaginative*."

"I wouldn't say that," Saundra replied. "You've come up with some great ideas for tour sites. Evan says you have a knack for knowing what draws in tourists and holds their interests."

"That's my job. I can make myself think like other people. I just can't think for myself," Callie joked. "And this morning my brain is really struggling. I think I slept about two hours before the alarm went off."

"Wow! The bridal shower lasted that long?"

It wasn't the shower, but the aftermath of it that had kept Callie flopping back and forth and punching her pillow in an effort to get comfortable.

Rubbing a hand across her pinched forehead, she said, "The shower ended at a reasonable hour. I had a sleepless night, that's all. Too much cake and punch, I suppose." Along with too much tall, dark and handsome, she thought.

Saundra looked at her. "I'll bet the shower was really something. The Ambling A ranch house is a mansion and the Abernathys go all-out with everything they do."

The Abernathys were a huge family with several branches. Even Evan Cruise and his sister Vanessa had recently learned they were related to the family through their grandmother Daisy who'd turned out to be the biological daughter of Josiah Abernathy.

Most of the Abernathys around Bronco

were extremely wealthy ranchers, but Callie didn't know whether that applied to Tyler and his branch of the family. He didn't seem like a man loaded with money. But appearances could be deceiving. Not that it mattered to her whether Tyler had a bulging bank account or was scraping the bottom of the barrel.

Callie replied, "Melanie received tons of gifts. Once she and Gabe are married, they won't have to buy a thing for their home."

"Ah, the rosy haze of love, the special plans and dreams," Saundra said cynically. "I hope it all lasts for them. Mine didn't. But, what the heck. I'm happy now."

Was she? Callie wanted to ask her, but didn't. Since Zach had ended things with Callie and moved away from Bronco, she'd experienced the sting of rejection and the loneliness that followed. She didn't know what had caused Saundra's divorce, but she figured the woman had suffered because of it.

Saundra reached into the box again. "There

are a few more things in here. Ghost Tour bookmarks, caps and journals. To write down all your ghostly experiences so you won't forget the details," she added jokingly. "Want to help me fix the window display? I thought we might drape some cobwebs and hang a few bats around. What can we use for a backdrop?"

Callie thought for a moment. "I got it. Somewhere in the storage room, there's a large poster of the old hotel that used to be in Bronco Heights years and years ago, before it burned to the ground. The building had a haunted look about it. In fact, I've heard some real tragic stories about its history. Even that a jilted lover caused the fire that destroyed it. Too bad it isn't still around. Bronco Ghost Tours would make a killing— pardon the pun—off of it."

Saundra's grin was wicked. "That sounds perfect! Let's go see if we can find the poster. Maybe we can have the display finished by the time Evan gets back from his meeting."

* * *

Tyler's watch showed half past noon when he parked his truck near Bronco Java and Juice and lifted Maeve from her safety seat. The popular eating spot would be especially busy at this time of day, but Tyler couldn't help the timing. He had not even expected to be in Bronco today. But the hay baler had suddenly stopped twining the bales, putting a pause on the whole project.

His father had sent Tyler into town to buy a part at the local tractor and farm machinery store to repair the problem. But the piece had to be ordered and wouldn't arrive until tomorrow.

After calling to give his father the disappointing news, Tyler had decided he might as well feed himself and Maeve before he drove back to the Flying A.

Inside the busy place, he found a vacant table not far from the juice bar. Once he'd situated Maeve in a high chair and a waitress had taken his order, he pulled a sippy cup from the baby's diaper bag and filled it with formula from a bottle.

The moment Maeve spotted the bottle in Tyler's hand, she began to whimper and reach for it. He quickly thrust the bottle back in the bag and offered the cup to the baby.

"No bottle right now, sweetheart," he gently explained to his daughter. "You're getting to be a big girl. You need to learn how to drink from your cup."

She protested with another loud whine before she decided the bright orange cup looked interesting and latched a tight grip around it. Relieved, Tyler helped her tilt the spout to her little lips.

"See, that's yummy. Just like your bottle," he said to the baby.

Maeve moved her mouth away from the spout and gave him a loud, happy coo and a grin that revealed one pearly tooth on her bottom gums.

Tyler was wondering if he was getting better at being a father or if Maeve was growing out of her tantrums, when he suddenly spotted Callie Sheldrick passing by a few steps from his table.

"Callie!"

Tyler didn't know what had made him call out to her, or even if he'd said her name loud enough for her to hear. But apparently she'd heard him because she suddenly paused and looked in his direction.

He glanced at Maeve to make sure she wasn't about to dump the sippy cup on top of her head, then stood and waited for Callie to reach his table.

Last night at the Ambling A, he'd noticed the pink dress she'd been wearing, but today he couldn't stop his gaze from slipping over the yellow-and-white dress skimming her slender figure. Nor could he stop wondering why a woman who looked as pretty and sweet as Callie was unattached. At least, Erica had told him that Callie wasn't married and didn't have a special guy on the string somewhere.

"Hi, Tyler. It's nice to see you again."

She was smiling and the cheery note in her voice warmed him.

Before he realized what he was doing, he was smiling back at her. "I'm glad to see you again, too," he said. "Are you having lunch or just a drink?"

"I'm having lunch with a coworker. Her treat, so I couldn't refuse," Callie told him. "I see you have a cute little lunch companion today."

She cast a tentative glance at Maeve, as though she feared the baby would start screaming angrily at any moment. Tyler couldn't blame her.

"I hadn't planned on being in town today, but I had to run an errand for Dad," Tyler told her. "The hay baler broke down. So instead of haying today, I'm here having lunch."

"Oh, that's too bad," she said. "I mean that your equipment had a breakdown. At least you'll have a nice lunch. The food here is great."

She darted a glance across the room to where a redheaded woman was sitting at a table, sipping a drink. Apparently she was the friend who was springing for Callie's lunch, Tyler decided.

"Well, I'll let you get back to your friend," he told her. "I, uh, just happened to see you and wanted to say hello."

"I'm glad that you did."

She looked happy to see him. Almost as happy as he was to see her.

Hell, what was coming over him? After the conversation he'd had with his brother last night, he'd decided his lot in life was to be alone. But now that she was standing only a few inches away and the corners of her lips were tilted into a charming smile, his thoughts were far from isolating himself in a lonely house.

"To tell you the truth, Callie, I, uh, was wondering if you'd like to have lunch with me. I have to return to town at this same time tomorrow and…" He paused as another thought struck him. "Oh, do you work on Saturdays?"

"I do. But I have an hour off for lunch."

"An hour would be fine," he told her. "That is—if you'd like to have lunch. We could meet here? Say, at twelve thirty?"

She studied him for a brief moment before saying, "That's fine with me. As long as you're sure about the invitation."

"Why wouldn't I be?" He inwardly groaned. Hell, he wasn't fooling Callie any more than he was fooling himself. The only thing he was sure about was that an unexpected need to spend time with her had struck him the moment he'd seen her walk by his table. And having lunch would be a perfectly harmless way to do it.

She shrugged then glanced uncertainly at Maeve. "I don't know."

Did she have an aversion to babies? Or was she truly concerned she might upset his daughter? Hoping it was the latter, he said, "I'm sure or I wouldn't have asked you."

A look of relief crossed her face. "Okay. Then I'll meet you here tomorrow."

He was so pleased she'd accepted his invitation that he reached across the table and wrapped his hand around hers. It felt as small and soft as it had last night and suddenly he was struck by the urge to lift the back of it to his lips. Where in the world was that coming from?

He cleared his throat, then said, "Good. I'll be here."

She glanced awkwardly over at her friend. "I, uh, think my lunch has been served. I'd better go eat before I have to go back to work."

"Oh. Sure." Realizing he was still holding her hand, he released it and eased back into his chair. "See you tomorrow."

"Yes, tomorrow."

Tyler watched her walk away, but once she reached the table where her coworker was seated, he didn't allow himself to glance in her direction. He'd already made himself look like a besotted fool. He didn't want her to catch him staring at her like a lost calf gazing across the pasture, searching for its momma.

* * *

"Who was that? I thought you'd forgotten all about your lunch! Your sandwich is probably cold now."

Callie felt so dazed, she reached for her cola and drew several sips through the straw before she answered Saundra's questions. "Sorry, Saundra. I didn't mean to be gone so long. On the way back from the restroom I, uh, ran into a…friend."

Saundra's brows shot up. "Friend? Do all your male friends hold your hand that way?"

Heat rushed to Callie's cheeks. "Don't be ridiculous. He was just giving me a polite goodbye."

Saundra looked far from convinced. "Well, I'll say one thing. He's quite a hunky cowboy. Who is he?"

Callie picked up a triangle of club sandwich. "An Abernathy. Tyler Abernathy, to be exact. I think he might be Gabe's cousin, or something like that."

Saundra's mouth formed a perfect O. "An Abernathy! This is getting more intriguing by the minute. And the baby with him, who does she belong to?"

"Maeve is his daughter."

The information left Saundra deflated. "The man is married. Shoot. I thought you might have found yourself a new guy."

Callie tried to laugh, but the sound was too garbled to resemble anything like amusement. "I'm not really looking for a new guy, Saundra. I'm still gluing myself back together from that fiasco with Zach. As for Tyler, he's a widower. His wife died in a highway accident about six months ago. I've been trying to remember hearing about the incident, but I don't. Do you recall anything about it?"

Saundra was shocked. "Oh my, how awful! Honestly, I don't remember anything about an Abernathy woman being killed in a car wreck, but you know me, I barely know what month we're in. Is this August?"

Callie swallowed a piece of the sandwich before she answered. "Yes, this is August. That means next month will be September."

Chuckling, Saundra forked up the last bite of chicken salad on her plate. "Right." Then she directed a coy glance at Callie. "So, Tyler Abernathy is single and available. Are you interested in him?"

Callie had spent half the night asking herself that same question and still wasn't sure about the answer. "I don't think so. Or maybe I would be interested if— Okay, Saundra, there's something about him that gets to me. But that doesn't necessarily mean anything." She absently jammed her straw down in the ice and cola. "I might as well tell you. You're going to hear about it anyway. He asked me to have lunch with him tomorrow and I accepted his invitation."

This time Saundra's eyebrows disappeared completely beneath the red fringe across her forehead. "Lunch? You and him? Callie, I'm stunned."

Callie drew in a long breath and let it out. Ever since she'd walked away from Tyler's table, she'd felt as if she was on a cloud, or a flying carpet, or something that was holding her feet off the floor.

"No more than I am," she admitted.

Saundra glanced over at Tyler's table, but Callie refused to follow the direction of her friend's curious gaze. The last thing she wanted was for Tyler to get the idea that she couldn't keep her eyes off him.

"Oh, how cute," Saundra remarked. "He's tied a bib on the baby and is feeding her something that looks like spinach or smashed-up green peas. I don't know any man who'd bother taking a child so young out to eat with him. Tyler must be special."

Purposely keeping her gaze fastened to her own plate, Callie said, "I have the impression that being a father is very important to him. Probably more important than anything."

"Well, that's a refreshing change. My ex never wanted children. That's how selfless he was," she said, her voice heavy with sarcasm.

Callie looked over at her. "Sorry, Saundra.

Is that why you two divorced? You wanted children and he didn't?"

"That was only a part of the reason. I'll tell you about it someday." She pointed to what was left of Callie's club sandwich. "Better finish your food. We only have ten minutes to get back to work."

While Callie hurriedly ate the last of her lunch, she had to fight to keep from looking over at Tyler and his daughter.

Was she crazy to get mixed up with a widower and his baby? What made her think she might help him move out of the tragic shadows of his past? It was stupid of her.

Don't fight it. Don't be afraid.

Suddenly, Winona's prophetic words whispered through her head. Had the old woman been talking about Callie and Tyler?

No! Most everyone considered Winona Cobbs just a little off-center. If the truth was known, she was probably as mystical as the black granite rock Callie used for a paperweight.

Besides, there wasn't really anything to fear. She and Tyler could never be anything more than friends.

for......and wondered if she'd never be anything more than a custodian...

Chapter Three

Callie had never been one to make much of a fuss over her appearance. But this morning she'd taken extra pains to pick something from her closet that wouldn't look too dressy, or so casual Tyler would think she was the custodian at Bronco Ghost Tours.

And if fretting over her clothes hadn't been enough, she'd spent a few more minutes trying to make her hair look smooth and sophisticated. A laughable idea with her naturally wavy hair that went berserk if the least bit of humidity moved in.

As she'd readied, Vanessa had paused in

the open doorway to Callie's bedroom and watched with a raised brow as she'd adjusted the belt on the cool denim skirt she'd chosen to wear. But thankfully her roommate hadn't commented on the skirt, or the white gauzy blouse she'd tucked into the waistband.

Callie hadn't told Vanessa about Tyler's lunch invitation. Mostly because she figured nothing would come out of the date. In fact, she was probably being presumptuous for even thinking it was a date.

By the time twelve thirty rolled around and Callie wheeled her little olive-green Jeep into a parking spot a few doors down from Bronco Java and Juice, she decided it didn't matter what sort of label she put on their meal together. Even if Tyler might be the tiniest bit interested in her, she might be wise not to get her hopes up. He was simply looking for female company. Not a wife.

Don't be a dope, Callie. Stop trying to figure out Tyler's motives. Just go enjoy the man.

Determined to follow the practical voice

in her head, she walked down the sidewalk to the coffee shop and was only a few steps away from the entrance when she heard Tyler's voice call out to her.

"Callie! Wait up!"

Pausing, she looked around to see him balancing Maeve in one arm and shutting the door on a black pickup with his free hand.

He's brought the baby with him. Why did that surprise her? Both times she'd seen the man, he'd had his daughter. That meant he probably took her with him whenever the occasion allowed. Still, the baby made it a threesome for lunch. And though Callie hated to admit it, the idea left her a bit wilted. All along, she'd been thinking she'd have the man to herself for one long hour.

"Perfect timing," he said as he joined her on the sidewalk. "We can go in together."

Callie was always wondering how it would feel to have a man at her side. Not a jerk like Zach, but a real man, the kind like Vanessa and Melanie had at their sides. Well, she couldn't see any harm in letting herself dream of Tyler being her man—for the next hour, at least.

She gave him a little smile. "I'm glad to see you, Tyler."

One corner of his lips lifted in a half grin and her heart reacted by doing a silly little somersault.

"So am I. I thought I was going to be late. I've been waiting for Dad's baler part to arrive." He shifted the baby to a more comfortable position in the crook of his left arm. "I hope you don't mind Maeve joining us today. I don't like leaving her with anybody else unless I absolutely have to."

The little girl was dressed adorably in a red-gingham shirt and tiny blue jeans. A red bow held her short curls in a cluster atop her head and Callie wondered if Tyler did all the baby's care by himself. It would be hard enough for a single man to deal with a son's needs, but a daughter would be an entirely different matter. How would a cowboy like Tyler know about hair bows and lacy dresses?

Realizing she hadn't made any sort of reply, she shook away her thoughts and said, "I don't mind. I admire you for taking your parental duties so seriously."

"Thanks," he said. Then taking her upper arm with his free hand, he urged her toward the entrance of the coffee shop. "Let's go on in. You only have an hour."

Since it was midday on a Saturday, Callie had expected the place to be busy, but she'd not imagined every table in the sunny dining area to be taken.

"Oh, looks like we're out of luck," she said. "There's no place to sit."

"We could go to the pizza place," he suggested. "But they don't have anything on the menu that Maeve can eat. What about going to a fast-food place for a burger?"

Callie was about to tell him that she was game for anything when she spotted a bus-boy clearing away the remnants of someone's meal.

"There's a table over by the window coming available," she told him. "Is it okay with you?"

"Great! Let's go snatch it before someone else does," he said.

With Tyler's hand gently resting against Callie's back, they crossed the room to where the busboy was wiping down the tabletop. Along the way, Callie sensed a few heads turning in their direction and it was more than clear that she wasn't the one arousing interest. The Abernathys, no matter what branch of the family, were well-known around Bronco. Especially in Bronco Heights where the upper crust of the town's population resided.

The busboy fetched a high chair for Maeve and, once the three of them were seated, a waitress appeared to take their order. After she left to get their drinks, Tyler pulled a teething ring from the diaper bag and gave it to Maeve. She immediately whammed the piece of rubber on the high chair tray then threw it on the floor.

Callie couldn't help but laugh at the baby's indignant protest. "I think she'd prefer food."

Grunting with amusement, he leaned over and picked up the teething ring. "Yeah, I insulted her. But she'll just have to wait. I have a sippy cup to give her, but I don't want her to get filled up with milk before the food arrives."

"I'd be at a total loss trying to do what you're doing," she admitted. "I've never been around babies much. A few of my friends have babies, but I've never held them."

"Why not?" he asked curiously. "You don't like kids?"

Callie wondered why this man had a special knack for making her blush. He seemed to ask all the awkward questions rather than the easy ones.

"Well, sure I do. I'd like to have children of my own someday. But I don't know enough about babies to feel comfortable caring for one yet," she admitted. Then hurriedly added, "But I'm a quick learner."

Doubt narrowed his eyes and her heart

sunk. She must have flunked the motherhood questions, no doubt a very important issue to him. But just as she was about to write off any chance of ever seeing him after today, a slow smile spread across his features. The expression lightened his blue eyes and softened the tense lines of his features. How nice it would be, she thought, if he smiled like that more often.

He said, "A quick learner is what you have to be around babies. Most of the time, I still don't know what I'm doing with Maeve. But I'm trying and doing the best I can."

"I'm sure you are. And that's all any of us can expect out of ourselves, don't you think?"

"Sometimes it's hard to give our best effort," he said solemnly. "And I fall short more than I succeed." He shrugged and cast her a wry smile. "But that's enough about that. Tell me about you. What do you do at Bronco Ghost Tours?"

She let out a soft laugh. "Technically, I'm Evan's assistant, but I do most anything that's needed around the office. I help with scheduling the tours. I explain to our customers how the tours are done and what the subject matter is. And I answer any questions they might have. We also sell Ghost Tour merchandise directly out of the store and online, so I help with that, too."

"Who actually guides the tours? Do you ever do that?"

A cacophony of sound filled the busy restaurant. Diners were laughing and talking, glasses clinked and cutlery rattled, while in the background, country music played. Yet the noise really wasn't registering with Callie. All she could hear was Tyler's low, masculine voice.

Shaking her head, she answered. "No, thank goodness. One time when Evan was in a pinch, he asked me to fill in. I was terrible at the job. But the guests were all nice and didn't seem to mind that I had to keep reading my notes.

"Evan started out guiding most of the tours, but things got so busy that he's hired two more guides to help. Molly's a middle-aged woman who also acts in a little theatre group here in town. She's extra good at dramatizing. And Josh, the other guide, is a young college student majoring in history. Talking about the town's old history is right up his alley."

"I can hear in your voice that you like your job," he said. "That's good. It's awful to be trapped in something that makes you miserable."

Was he talking about himself or about people in general? She started to ask him, but Maeve chose that moment to start pounding her fist against her chair tray.

He fished out another plastic toy and was trying to distract the baby when the waitress suddenly arrived with their food.

Minutes later, Maeve was happily cramming soft finger foods into her mouth and making goo-gaa noises at her daddy.

Callie delicately picked at her salad, while Tyler worked his way through a Rueben sandwich and a mountain of french fries.

"I'd like to hear about your job, Tyler," she said. "Do you like ranching?"

"Very much. My dad, Hutch, has always been a rancher and that's how he raised me and my four brothers. He built the Flying A—that's our ranch. Or maybe you already knew that?"

"No. I'm acquainted with a few Abernathys and, of course, I know the Ambling A, but I don't believe I've heard the Flying A mentioned. There are so many of you Abernathys here in Bronco. Your family is so huge."

"And getting bigger every day," he replied with a grin. "I think I've lost count of all my cousins."

"I recall your brothers were the ones helping you run the Abernathy Meats booth at the Fourth of July celebration."

Nodding, he said, "That was all five of us—Dean, Garrett, Weston, Crosby and me. I have a separate house on my parents' property. So does Dean. All of us guys are ranchers and we work with Dad to keep everything running and profitable."

"The winters can be brutal here in Montana," she said thoughtfully. "Working outdoors during those months has to be tough."

"We're all acclimatized to the extreme temperatures. And if calving happens during a spell of bad weather, we're too busy seeing after the cows and calves to pay much attention to the snow or rain, electrical storm or whatever the case may be."

"Oh my. You must be tough. I freeze whenever I run from my apartment to my car just to get to work."

He chuckled. "You have to wear plenty of thermal underwear, wool socks and an oiled duster when the rain comes. It wouldn't look quite as pretty as what you're wearing today, but you'd be warm."

He thought her blouse and skirt were pretty? The idea was enough to make her glow inside.

"Ooooeee! Aaaggaa!"

Maeve's happy squeal had them both glancing over to see the baby smearing a piece of banana on the top of her head.

"Oh, Maeve!" Tyler exclaimed with a groan. "You're supposed to be eating that banana. It's fruit, not a hair ornament!"

Callie tried not to laugh. "Well, once it dries, it will act like setting gel and hold her curls in place."

He shot her a dry look before he chuckled. "You would think like a girl."

"Naturally."

He grabbed up a napkin and tried to wipe most of the gooey fruit from Maeve's hair and hands.

"At least she's happy," he said. "It's much easier to clean her up than to stop her crying."

Callie couldn't help noticing how gentle he was with the baby, even when she was fussing or making a mess. It made her wonder if he'd learned those parenting skills from his late wife or if they'd come to him naturally. She'd heard that, contrary to their rugged looks, cowboys were usually gentle and softhearted. Maybe because they worked so closely with nature and saw firsthand how animals nurtured their babies. Whatever the case, Tyler seemed to have the touch.

"Do your brothers have children, too?" she asked.

He let out a short laugh as he offered another piece of banana to his daughter. This time the baby decided to eat it rather than use it for pomade.

"No," he said. "I'm the only one who has a child. Garrett was married once, but he's divorced. Dean, Crosby and Weston have never been married."

That surprised her. "Where are you in the birth order? The oldest?"

With another laugh, he forked up a fry doused in melted cheese before he popped it into his mouth. "I'm twenty-eight and the baby of the family."

"I'm the baby of my family, too," she told him. "I'm twenty-five and I have an older sister, Dakota."

"Does she live in Bronco?"

"No. She lives in Cheyenne. With her boyfriend. I live here with my roommate, Vanessa Cruise. My boss's sister. But I don't expect her to be staying in the apartment much longer. She and Jameson John will probably be getting married sooner rather than later."

"I know Jameson, but I don't see him often. As for Vanessa and Evan, most of us Abernathys were surprised as heck when it turned out their grandmother Daisy was actually Josiah Abernathy and Winona Cobbs's daughter. Guess that makes those two related to me and my brothers as some degree of cousins, or something like that."

Callie shook her head. "It amazes me that there are so many branches to the Abernathy tree. My family is small. Just me and my sister and parents. My mom's parents retired to Florida, so we rarely see them, and Dad's folks both passed away at an early age. I think we might have a couple of cousins through our dad's side, but we've never met them. You see, Dad's brother entered the navy when he was very young and ended up making his home in Virginia."

"What do your parents do?"

Was he actually interested in her family? Or was he just being polite? She wanted to think the former. Especially when he was the only guy who'd ever made a point to ask about her parents.

Warmed by that thought, she said, "My mom, Patricia, works in Bronco Heights as an administrative assistant for an insurance broker. And my dad, Martin, is a carpenter. He works for a local construction company."

He grinned. "And I'll bet they're very proud of you, Callie."

She felt her cheeks turn pink as she tried to laugh off his compliment. "I don't know about that. They were proud I managed to get a business degree in college. But I think they were planning on me having a more traditional job. Bronco Ghost Tours isn't exactly an average sort of business."

"No," he said thoughtfully. "But apparently it makes Evan a living and you and your co-workers like it. Something being traditional doesn't always mean it's the best."

He was feeding her ego and she wondered how and where she could find any man around Bronco who could make her feel the warmth and happiness that Tyler was giving her at this very moment.

To her, it felt like the lunch had just started when Tyler suggested they finish up so she wouldn't be late getting back to work.

After he'd paid the bill and they'd walked along the sidewalk to where his truck was parked, she tried not to feel disheartened that her time with Tyler was over.

"Thank you so much for lunch, Tyler. It was very nice."

He smiled at her. "Even with Maeve turning her hair into a banana split?"

Callie chuckled. "Maeve was adorable. And now it looks like she's about to fall asleep on your shoulder. Her eyes are very nearly closed."

"She'll sleep all the way back to the ranch." He glanced at Maeve then turned his eyes back on Callie. "I, uh, enjoyed this today, Callie. I don't do any socializing. The shower the other night was the first party I've been to in—well, a long time."

A long time. In other words, since his wife died. All throughout their lunch, Callie had noticed that he'd never once mentioned losing his wife or even said her name. It was rather sad to think it was too painful for him to talk about her, even in an offhand way. But maybe he felt like he hadn't known Callie long enough to talk about his private life.

"I'm glad you enjoyed it."

He glanced at his watch then looked up at her again. "I was thinking… Uh, before you leave, I wanted to ask if you'd like to go out for dinner one night."

Her jaw very nearly dropped. Tyler Abernathy was asking her out to dinner? Lunch was one thing, but this sounded like a real date!

"Dinner? I'd love to." She probably sounded far too eager, but she hardly saw any point in acting coy. What little she'd been around him, she had gotten the impression that he was a man who appreciated frankness from a woman, not silly games.

A pleased expression suddenly lit up his face and the sight sent Callie's spirits straight into the blue sky.

"I'm glad. Real glad," he said. "And don't worry, I'll try to find someone to watch Maeve."

Instinct pushed her forward until she was close enough to place a hand on his forearm. "Tyler, Maeve is a part of you. I could never resent her. I might not know how to interact with her, but I can learn."

Relief washed over his face, followed by a wry smile. "Yes, you can. When Maeve was born, I was totally clueless about babies. Over the months, she's taught me how to be a dad. I'm grateful to you for understanding about her."

The man needs me.

The signal is strong.

Oh Lord, those strange thoughts were rolling through her head again. What had Winona Cobbs done to her?

Pushing the crazy question from her mind, she asked, "When did you want to have dinner?"

He didn't flounder about answering, "Tomorrow night would be good for me. What about you?"

She'd expected him to say a few days or even a week from now. Not one day! Had she stepped into some sort of wondrous dream from which she'd wake at any moment?

Trying to hide her surprise, she said as casually as she could, "Oh sure. Tomorrow night would be fine."

"Good. I'll pick you up at seven." He pulled a cell phone from his pocket. "You'd better give me your address and phone number."

He tapped in the information she provided and followed the task with a quick goodbye.

"See you tomorrow night," he called to her as he carried Maeve to his waiting truck.

"Yes. Tomorrow night." Callie waved him

off and then forced herself not to skip and dance her way along the sidewalk to her Jeep.

"Mom, you're a gem for watching Maeve tonight."

Inside the kitchen of his parents' ranch house, Tyler placed Maeve's bag of necessities on the end of a long counter and then stepped over to where his tall, auburn-haired mother was ladling leftovers into a plastic container.

"Give that precious little darling to me." A wide smile on her face, Hannah held her arms toward her one and only grandchild. "I'm never too busy for my girl."

Tyler handed the baby over to his mother and, instantly, Maeve cooed and patted her grandmother's face. Hannah had always known how to put a happy face on Maeve. After raising five sons, she was a natural with babies, and while Luanne had been alive and struggling to deal with Maeve's constant crying, Hannah had tried to help her daughter-in-law. But Luanne had resented her offers.

She'd wanted Hannah, and everyone else, to believe that her mothering skills were above reproach. And to add insult to injury, Luanne had told Hannah that she'd already raised her own babies and that Maeve was none of her business.

Tyler had been furious over his wife's hateful behavior, but he'd been caught in an awkward spot between the two women. Understanding the situation, his mother, being the diplomat of the family, had kindly held her tongue. After that, Hannah had never offered to help with the baby again. She'd given up the joy of being with her new little granddaughter just to make Luanne happy.

Damn it, for over five years, he tried to make his wife happy. In the end, he'd failed miserably.

The sound of his mother laughing and smacking kisses on Maeve's face pulled him out of his dark thoughts and he smiled as the baby shrieked with laughter.

Hannah turned her attention to her son. "You can't imagine how good it makes me feel to see you dressed up like this. And going out with a young woman, too. I'm proud of you for making this effort, Ty."

He couldn't figure why the thought of being with Callie filled him with happy anticipation, or what it was about her that charmed him. Looking at her and experiencing that pull of attraction was like he'd been risen from the dead. Yet there was part of him that felt extremely guilty for letting himself feel those pleasures again.

"Having dinner with Callie is just that, Mom. Nothing more. She's just someone I met at Mel and Gabe's shower."

She angled him a knowing look. "There must've been something about the girl that prompted you to ask her for a date. Is she pretty?"

These past few days, Tyler had been trying to figure out what it was about Callie that he found attractive. One look at Luanne and anyone could've guessed why she'd turned

Tyler's head. Her blond, blue-eyed looks had flashed in his eyes like the city lights where she'd been born and raised. She'd been alluring and sexy, and at twenty-two years of age, he'd been ripe and ready for a woman like her. But it was nothing like that with Callie. She had a gentle beauty. One that had slowly reached out and taken hold of him.

"Callie is pretty in a quiet way. She has dark hair and brown eyes, and she's tiny. She comes to about here." He measured a spot in the middle of his chest. "But more than any of that, she's easy to talk to."

Nodding, Hannah said, "That's good. Because you haven't done a whole lot of talking since Luanne died."

His mother couldn't have been more right. For the past six months, he'd had to force himself to utter a few words at a time, much less string several sentences together. He realized his friends and family had all become frustrated with his grunts and single-word responses, but he hadn't wanted to communicate with anyone.

"I haven't wanted to talk," he admitted. "Talking takes a lot of thought and effort, and I don't have much of either."

Ignoring that, Hannah carried Maeve over to a high chair situated at one end of a long, polished-pine breakfast table.

"I didn't see Dad anywhere in the house when I came in. Where is he, anyway? Out in the barn?"

Hannah said, "Some rancher south of town has a bull for sale that Hutch thought he might want to buy for the Flying A. He went to take a look at him."

Tyler shot her a look of concern. His parents were far from elderly. In fact, at the age of sixty-four, both were fit and vibrant. Even so, Tyler worried when either went out driving at night. He realized his fears resulted from Luanne's accident, but acknowledging the reason wasn't enough to make it go away.

"I hope he didn't go alone. The elk are still down on the flats and they wander onto the highway. If—"

"Ty, stop worrying. Dean is with him.

They'll be careful. Besides, the last thing you need to be doing is worrying about your dad or brothers. Or, for that matter, little Maeve. You go enjoy yourself with your date."

Sighing, he pushed up the slide on his bolo tie. "Yeah, and quit being paranoid."

He placed a kiss on Maeve's forehead and started out of the kitchen, but another thought had him pausing at the door and looking back at his mother.

"Mom, do you think people are going to see me out with Callie and think I'm being disrespectful to Luanne?"

Frowning, she walked over to him and laid a hand on his upper arm. "Oh, Tyler, no matter what you do, people are going to think and say things. The moment Luanne died, that part of your life ended. Days, months, years—no amount of passing time will change that. You have to quit dwelling in the past and, when you do, you'll understand that you have to live for you—not anyone else."

He gave her a lopsided grin. "How did I manage to get a mother like you?"

"Just lucky, I guess." She kissed his cheek, then gently shoved him out the door. "Get out of here. You don't want to keep that woman waiting."

Callie was dropping a few extra items into her handbag when a knock announced Tyler's arrival.

Her heart racing, she smoothed her dress down the sides of her hips and walked quickly to the door of her ground-floor apartment.

A quick peek through the peephole confirmed it was Tyler and she quickly opened the door and pushed it wide enough for him to enter.

"Hi, Tyler. Won't you come in? I'm almost ready."

"I'm a few minutes' early," he said. "I hope you don't mind?"

He stepped past her and into a hallway that doubled as a foyer. As Callie shut the door behind him, she tried not to gape at him.

There was no mistaking that he considered tonight a date. He was dressed in dark jeans, a Western-cut shirt with pearl snaps, and a bolo tie with a slide made from a turquoise stone. His dark waves were damp and tousled in a sexy way and a hint of spicy aftershave drifted from his newly shaved face.

"Uh, no. I don't mind. Do we have enough time for me to show you my apartment?" she asked.

"Sure. I'd like to see it."

She motioned for him to follow.

After they'd taken a few steps down the hall, she gestured to an open doorway to their left. "The kitchen is in here. Let's go through and we'll come out on the other side to the living room."

"This is cozy," he said as he eyed the row of cabinets and the bright yellow-and-white curtain hanging over the single window. "Do you and your roommate do much cooking?"

Callie's laugh was sheepish. "I have to confess, Tyler. I know very little about cooking." She walked over to a small microwave and patted the top of it. "If not for this thing, I'd probably starve. Van cooks, but she's not always here."

He glanced at a peninsula that separated the kitchen from the living room. "Is Vanessa not here now?"

"No. She's out with Jameson somewhere," Callie told him. "They spend as much time together as possible. You know how it is."

"Yeah," he said dolefully. "I know how it is."

As soon as he answered, it dawned on Callie that she'd spoken without thinking. Embarrassed heat rushed to her cheeks. "Oh, excuse me, Tyler, I shouldn't have said that."

Shaking his head, he moved over to where she was standing and Callie realized this was the first time she'd ever seen him without Maeve. It seemed a little strange, as though part of him was missing.

"It was the truth. When two people are in love, they want to be together. Listen, Callie, I'm a widower, but that doesn't mean you have to weigh every word that comes out of your mouth. I don't want you to be miserable around me."

She let out a breath of relief. "Thank you, Tyler, for being understanding about it. I've always been the girl who puts her foot in her mouth. If I start making a habit of it tonight, just put some tape over my lips."

His gaze fell to her lips and Callie felt her whole mouth begin to tingle with anticipation. How would it feel to have this man kiss her? Would she ever know? Or had he lost the desire to be emotionally involved with a woman?

The questions were rolling around in her head when he moved a few steps away from her to stand near the small farm table and four chairs where she and Vanessa ate their meals.

"I think you'd have a hard time trying to eat with tape over your lips." He glanced curiously around the breakfast nook then out toward the living room. "Have you lived here long?"

"A couple of years or something like that.

Long before I started working for Evan at Bronco Ghost Tours. That was back in November of last year. And then at Christmas I—" She looked away and, for the second time already this evening, wished she'd kept her mouth shut.

"You what?" he prompted.

Forcing herself to turn her gaze back to him, she did her best to smile as though she wasn't about to recount one of the most humiliating times of her life.

"I broke up with my boyfriend, or he broke up with me. Doesn't make much difference which one of us actually did the breaking. The end arrived—and right before Christmas. To make matters worse, my parents were out of town at the time. Evan felt so awful about me being alone at Christmas that he kindly invited me to spend the holiday with his family. Vanessa didn't move in with me until this summer when she moved here from Billings."

His blue eyes narrowed with speculation.

"What about your boyfriend? Is he still around?"

"Ex-boyfriend," she corrected. "And no, he left Bronco Valley and went off to Kalispell or somewhere. I don't really know or care. We're finished."

Leaning a hip against the edge of the table, he folded his arms against his chest as though they had all the time in the world.

"What happened?" he asked. "Did the guy have a roving eye? Or is that question too personal?"

Callie shrugged, thinking if she could open up to him, he might eventually want to share some of his past with her.

"I was never aware of Zach having other women on the side. That wasn't the problem. He was the possessive sort and when Bronco Ghost Tours got busier and busier, and I had to start putting in long hours on the job, he resented my job. Because I wasn't spending enough time with him, he was insulted, indignant, infuriated. I'm sure you get the picture."

He chuckled. "I do. It took plenty of *I* words to describe the guy."

She laughed. "Right. But eventually, after I'd had time to think on it, I realized I was better off without him. Zach was a me, me, me person. And, anyway, I'm still young and I happen to believe that someday my prince will come along."

The smile on his face faded. "Is that what you want? A prince?"

Her heart was suddenly pounding and she wasn't sure why. Maybe because there wasn't much space between the two of them and she could feel the heat radiating from his hard body. Or maybe it was the intensity of his blue eyes as they delved into hers. Whatever the reason, he was creating upheaval inside her.

"That was only a figure of speech. I don't want a prince. I want a normal guy who will love me and give me a family. That's all."

"That's all? That's a lot," he said as though she was asking for the moon and stars.

"I suppose. So far, the boyfriends I've had

were all determined to remain single." She shrugged and did her best to smile. "Van says I'm a hopeless romantic. That I let infatuation blind me so that I don't see a guy's faults. She could be right. But sometimes you have to look around the flaws to see the good parts of a person. Don't you think?"

"We all have our faults. Some more than others."

Were those sad shadows she saw in his blue eyes? Or was it the kitchen lighting that caused his expression to suddenly sober? Whatever the case, she decided it was past time to move on from the subject of boyfriends and love, and her lack of both.

"Come on," she said. "I'll show you the rest of the apartment."

He followed her past the dining table and into a larger room furnished with a brown couch, a pair of copper-colored stuffed armchairs, and a glass-and-wood coffee table. On the outer wall, a large picture window framed a view of a grassy courtyard surrounded on three sides by the apartment complex.

"This is where we kick back and relax. It's nothing fancy, but it's comfortable," she said as he made a slow perusal of the room.

He walked over to the window. "Nice view. Far better than staring out at a busy street."

"The window is probably my favorite part of the apartment. I like looking out at the courtyard. On most days, kids are playing on the grass and there's a park bench beneath the shade tree. Whenever I have time, I go out there with a handful of seeds and nuts to feed the squirrels and birds."

"You like the outdoors?"

The doubt in his voice didn't make sense. Did he think just because she lived in town that she preferred concrete beneath her feet and the comfort of being indoors? Could it be that his late wife hadn't liked the outdoors? Callie could ask him, but she sensed he wouldn't appreciate her raising the subject. Besides, she wasn't sure she wanted to hear him talk about the woman he'd loved and cherished. Not tonight, anyway.

"I love the outdoors. I used to be sort of a tomboy. I liked to climb trees and play baseball with the boys. And fishing with my dad. That's something I still like to do. I was probably halfway through elementary school before I actually wanted to wear a dress."

He grinned and Callie wondered how one little expression on his face could cause her knees to feel like wet sponges.

"And now?" he asked.

Chuckling softly, she said, "Now the days of playing outside in the sun are over. I had to grow up and get a job to support myself." She pointed down the hallway that continued past the living room. "There are two bedrooms down the hall, a main bathroom at the end of it, and a half bath in one of the bedrooms. That makes it nice for Van and me. We don't have to fight for a bathroom. Especially when we're in a hurry to get to work."

He took a quick look down the hallway as Callie picked up her handbag from the sofa.

"Ready to go?" she asked.

He glanced at his watch. "By the time we get there, it'll be time for our reservation. And I don't know about you, but I'm getting hungry. Are you?"

"I'm always hungry," she replied, wondering where he'd be taking her that would require reservations. All of Callie's past boyfriends had been the pizza and fast-food sort. Once in a while, Zach had sprung for a chicken-fried steak, but that had been the height of her dining experiences with him. Reservations were for people like the Taylors or Daltons. Or the Abernathys. Not for folks like Callie.

Callie did her best to ignore the uncomfortable thought as the two of them left the apartment. This was a special night for her. She wasn't going to ruin it by analyzing the differences between her and Tyler.

When they reached his truck, he helped

her into the cab. After he'd seated himself behind the steering wheel, he glanced over at her. "In case you're wondering, we're going to DJ's Deluxe and the reservation isn't until eight. That's why I wasn't in a big rush to leave your apartment."

"DJ's Deluxe! But I've heard you often have to wait a month to get reservations to that place. How did—"

"I manage to get a table? You're probably going to find this hard to believe, but I happened to call at the right time. They'd just had a cancellation."

Timing or luck, either way Callie was impressed he'd managed to get a table tonight. "I've heard the food is scrumptious. But I wouldn't know. I've never been there."

If her admission surprised him, he didn't show it. Probably out of politeness, she decided.

"They have a long menu to choose from and everything on it is delicious. But if you'd feel more comfortable going somewhere else, it won't bother me to cancel the reservation."

Before she could stop it, a soft laugh escaped her lips. "Tyler, you see that I live in the Valley. Anytime I have a chance to eat in the Heights it's a real treat. But I never expected you to spend so much on our dinner. I can eat pizza or whatever you like."

His eyes wandered down the soft blue jersey dress that draped her curves and exposed the tiniest hint of cleavage. "I don't know much about women's fashions, but that doesn't look like something you throw on to go eat pizza."

Oh Lord, had she overdone it? She'd wanted to look nice. But she hadn't wanted him to think she was trying too hard. And she'd picked out the dress not knowing where they'd be eating.

She turned her attention away from him and focused on fastening the seat belt across her lap. "I can eat anything in this dress. Even packaged sandwiches out of the convenience store."

For the first time since she'd met him, he laughed outright, and the sound was full of genuine amusement. It was a very nice sound, she decided. One that she hoped she heard again.

"I think I can do a bit better than that." He reached over and clasped his hand around hers. "But you're sweet to offer, Callie. Very sweet."

His hand was work-worn tough, but it was warm and reassuring, while the look in his blue eyes melted her very bones. Going out with Tyler tonight was turning out to be far riskier to her heart than she'd first imagined.

"And you're very nice to give me such a special dinner, Tyler," she told him. "Thank you."

He studied her face for a long moment before he released her hand and turned to start the engine.

When he finally backed the truck onto the street and headed in the direction of Bronco Heights, Callie could only wonder why she'd ever had the foolish thought that Tyler Abernathy needed her.

He was a man who had everything. Except his late wife. And Callie couldn't replace her. She wouldn't even want to try.

Chapter Four

There was something happening between him and Callie, Tyler decided. And it had nothing to do with the wine they were having with their dinner. No, it felt far more magical than anything manifested from a bit of alcohol. But how long would the feeling last? Would this connection between them end once they left the restaurant?

Tyler had no idea what would happen when they walked out of DJ's Deluxe and he took her home. But he did know one thing. He didn't want this special feeling to end. At least, not for a while.

"I've never tasted beef like this," Callie said as she sliced off a piece of the prime rib on her plate. "It melts in my mouth. And the flavor is out of this world."

From the moment they'd entered the restaurant, he'd noticed Callie glancing appreciatively at the rich wood tables and bar, where a busy bartender was mixing cocktails. And even though she'd not commented on the burgundy wine Tyler had ordered with their meal, he'd observed how she was savoring each sip. The fact that she was enjoying herself made him feel happier than he'd felt in a long time.

Luanne had been miserable most of their married life. Dining at DJ's Deluxe had meant nothing to her. She'd expected the best from him and when she hadn't gotten it, she was quick to express her displeasure. Most men would've never put up with his late wife's demands, but Tyler had felt guilty for keeping her in Montana, so he'd looked the other way. It hadn't been until after her death that he'd begun to realize the mistakes he'd made as a husband.

He'd made wrong choices in an effort to please Luanne. But as Callie's date tonight, he felt sure he was doing something right. There was a gentle, warm smile on her face that radiated deep into his soul, waking parts of him laid dormant these past dark months.

"I'm glad you're enjoying it." He gestured toward her plate. "What about your baked potato? You've hardly touched it."

She laughed. "Tyler, are you sure we're not in Texas instead of Montana? Look at the size of that thing! I'll do well to eat a fourth of it. And it's melt-in-your-mouth delicious, too."

Taking a sip from his wineglass, he allowed his gaze to slip over her dark hair. A wave dipped near her right eye and each time she moved her head the shiny curtain swished against the top of her shoulders. Oddly, he'd never thought himself attracted to dark-haired women. Yet Callie's hair was like soft brown silk and, when he stood close to her, he could smell the faint scent of flowers drifting from it.

"You need to save room for dessert," he told her. "A meal like this isn't complete without something to satisfy your sweet tooth."

She pulled an impish face at him and Tyler realized it had been ages since he'd exchanged this sort of lighthearted banter with anyone.

"Hmm. How do you know I have a sweet tooth?" she asked mischievously.

"Just a guess. You look like a chocolate girl to me."

She shot him a playful frown. "Are you related to Winona Cobbs?"

He chuckled. "Probably by marriage in some distant way. Why?"

"Because you obviously have mystic powers. You knew I loved chocolate."

With another chuckle, he shook his head. "That's not mystic powers, Callie. That's a natural conclusion. Most women love chocolate."

"Aw, and here I thought I'd found another

Bronco psychic," she teased. Then she changed the subject. "How is little Maeve? Is she staying with a relative tonight?"

The fact that she asked about his daughter pleased him more than she could possibly guess. The night of the shower when Maeve had burst out crying, Callie had looked so horrified, Tyler had thought she must surely have an aversion to kids. Now that he was getting to know her, he could see she was simply inexperienced with babies.

"She's at my parents' house. Mom is watching her."

Callie dug into the mound of baked potato smothered in sour cream and chives. "I'll bet your mother is great with kids. She'd have to be after having five sons."

Tyler nodded. "Growing up, all of us boys were rascals. I don't know how our parents survived our younger years. But somehow we grew out of being pranksters and turned into responsible adults."

She looked at him. "Does working with your dad ever cause a problem? I love my daddy dearly, but the times that I've tried to help him with his carpentry work, we'd always end up in a big argument. I could never hold the board just right or drive the nail in the right place."

He couldn't imagine Callie doing carpentry work. She was so soft and feminine. Sometimes when he looked at her, he found himself wondering if living on a ranch would be too rough for her.

Damn it. He didn't know why such a question would enter his brain. He didn't want another wife. The hell he'd gone through with Luanne had slammed the door shut on his heart. He wasn't sure he could ever love another woman deeply enough to want her to be his wife.

Shaking that thought away, he said, "Working with family can get touchy. Especially when you're as close as I am to my brothers and dad. More often than not, we speak our minds before we think. On the other hand, we're all quick to forget and forgive. So everything works out."

"Must be nice," she said wistfully. "I wish my sister lived closer to me. I miss having her company and sharing my ups and downs with her. The two of us aren't really that much alike. She's an RN and very brainy. But she understands me and I get what she's all about."

"Do you ever go to Wyoming to visit her?"

"I haven't in a long while. Traveling is expensive. And I'm so tied up at Bronco Ghost Tours I do well to get my laundry done on the weekends. Much less drive over to Wyoming."

She'd already admitted that her boyfriend had skipped out on her because of the long hours she'd spent on the job. The situation she'd described was similar to what had taken place with him and Luanne. He'd buried himself in ranch work, staying out till late at night. Most of it had been legitimate chores. Yet there'd been times he'd created tasks just so he wouldn't have to face his unhappy wife and crying baby. He was guilty of that and so much more, he thought glumly.

But when he looked at Callie's smiling face, he desperately wanted to believe he could push all that guilt away and look to the future.

Nearly an hour later, after they'd finished a dessert of rich turtle brownies topped with whipped cream and accompanied with cups of strong coffee, Tyler drove back to her apartment complex and parked in a slot designated for guests.

When he shut off the motor, her heart thudded with anticipation. The evening had been so enchanting for Callie that she didn't want it to end. But she could only guess as to whether Tyler felt the same way. Especially when he had yet to utter one word.

Desperate to break the silence, Callie said, "I can't remember the last time I ate so much. I'm stuffed."

"Me, too."

Callie unfastened her seat belt and glanced over at him. There was a distant expression on his face, as though he was somewhere other than sitting next to her. Even so, she decided not to let his preoccupation squash her desire to keep this time with him going. At least, for a few more minutes.

"Would you like to come in for a while?" she asked. "Or we could sit out under the tree. The evening is still warm."

Her suggestion seemed to snap him out of his thoughts and he gave her a nod. "Outside sounds good," he replied. "These warm August nights won't last much longer. We need to enjoy them."

They departed the truck and, with a hand against her back, Tyler guided her to the courtyard. As they strolled over the freshly clipped grass, Callie was reminded of how alone she'd felt these past several months.

Since Zach had skedaddled out of Bronco, she'd watched most of her friends find love, get engaged and even get married. She'd tried not to lose faith and feel like the poor little girl standing on the outside, peering in the castle window. However, as the days and weeks had passed without finding her prince, her spirits had started to flag. But, for tonight, with Tyler walking at her side, she felt as though she was floating among the stars.

"Looks like we have the place to ourselves," Tyler said when they reached the concrete bench.

"Everyone is probably inside watching TV." Using her hand, she brushed off a spot in the middle of the bench then sat.

Tyler joined her and she was acutely aware that mere inches separated their legs.

"I didn't see a TV in your living room," he remarked. "Do you and Vanessa not watch television?"

"Only if there's something special we want to see. But we don't have a TV. We just stream off our laptops."

"Oh, the two of you are uptown girls," he jokingly mused.

She chuckled. "You're forgetting we live in Bronco Valley. We'd have to be in Bronco Heights to actually be uptown."

He directed a curious gaze at her. "Would you rather be living in the Heights?"

Callie shook her head. "Not really. I feel fortunate to be living where I am—doing what I do. There are some very wealthy families living in and around Bronco. The Abernathys, the Taylors, and Daltons, and I happen to be friends with some of them, including you. But I don't covet the rich, if that's the point of your question."

"Hmm. Don't put me in that rich category, Callie. Yes, we Abernathys own the Flying A Ranch, and our finances our comfortable, but we're not wildly wealthy like some of our relatives."

As Callie's gaze thoughtfully slipped over his face, she realized he was very different than any man she'd ever dated. He was far more complex and mature. Perhaps that came from being a husband and a single father. And a widower.

"We talked about lots of things during dinner, but not much about your job on the ranch. I don't know much about cowboy things or raising livestock. I guess you rope and ride, but what else do you do?"

"At present, we're working on getting all the hay meadows cut and baled. We try to grow enough to last through the winter. But that's always iffy. If the rains don't come, hay is scarce, along with any winter grazing. To make it even harder to calculate what we'll need in the way of feed and grain, we never know how bad the winter might be. If blizzards hit, we have to practically double the amount of hay and up the feed."

"I see," she said thoughtfully. "So much of ranching depends on the weather."

He nodded. "Exactly. And we have no control over what Mother Nature gives us."

"I'd be walking the floor and chewing my nails," she admitted then asked, "What else do you do, other than the haying?"

He frowned. "Are you sure you want to hear this sort of thing?"

"Sure I'm sure. The Bronco area has many ranches. I need to learn about the business.

You never know, Evan might decide to offer a ranching tour in the near future."

"Yes, but ranching isn't exactly a subject you discuss on a date."

She gave him a lopsided grin. "Maybe that should depend on who you're dating."

"As I look at you right now—I'm not thinking about ranching. You look...all woman."

Callie didn't know what was happening to her, but from the moment they'd sat on the bench, her senses had dialed in to every tiny thing about the man. From his spicy scent, to the low, sexy timbre of his voice, everything about him was sending erotic signals to her brain. And the way he was gazing at her— like a man did when he wanted a woman— was making every private place on her body hum with need.

She let out a shaky laugh in the hope of hiding the fact that she was melting inside. "I might look girlie, but, uh, I'd still like to hear about your work. Is haying and feeding most everything you do?"

"That's only a fraction of the jobs we do on

the ranch. Fence mending goes on all year 'round. The same goes for checking on the cattle to make sure none are sick or injured or stuck in a mud hole.

"In the spring, we have roundup and branding. In the fall, we wean the calves and drive them to separate pastures. When the calves begin to drop in late winter, we really get busy. Sometimes we have to give the mothers extra help to give birth. Sometimes the newborns aren't breathing and we have to work to try to save them. And then we have to worry about the young calves getting dysentery. That can be deadly and, if it happens, we have to go around doctoring them with medication. On those occasions, it's not uncommon for us to work through the night. There are many more things we do, along with plenty of other full-time chores. Sound boring?"

She laughed. "Are you kidding? I don't know how you drag yourself out of bed in the mornings."

Amused by her comment, he said, "Like

anyone else. You crack your eyes open and swing your legs to the floor, then stumble to the kitchen to guzzle down a few cups of coffee."

"A few cups," she repeated with a groan of disbelief. "After all you just told me, I'd need a gallon."

"Do you normally get up early enough to drink coffee before work?" he asked.

His question made her wonder if his late wife had lazed around in the mornings. Or maybe he was thinking Callie was the sluggish sort.

"I get up early," she told him. "Especially when we have a busy day of tours scheduled. I like to get to the office before the day starts rolling so I can double-check departure times of the tours and make sure none overlap. The gift shop has to be restocked nearly every morning, too. We sell a ton of merchandise."

His smile was wry. "I'm sorry, Callie, but when I think of people taking tours of haunted places and spooks, I—"

"Want to laugh?" she finished for him.

Grinning sheepishly, he said, "Maybe not laugh, but roll my eyes. To be honest, when I heard Evan was putting in a ghost tour business, I thought it might last a month or two. I couldn't imagine anyone wanting to tour haunted places. If there really are such places," he added skeptically.

She slanted him an indulgent look. "Depends on the person. Some people get goose bumps just hearing about haunted places or scary incidents. And some laugh at the whole idea of a ghost and goblins."

Smiling faintly, he reached over and slid his fingers up and down her forearm. "What about you, Callie? Do you get goose bumps?"

Her heart suddenly decided it needed to run instead of walk. "I, uh, the thought of a ghost doesn't do anything to me," she murmured. "When it comes to spooky things, I guess I must be numb."

His head bent slightly toward hers and Callie wondered why the tree limbs appeared to be swaying when there was no wind. And why were the stars streaking across the sky like comets with long bright tails?

"I don't believe you're numb, Callie. You feel soft and warm and very alive. And I... um, think—" He pulled his hand back from her arm and rose from the bench. "I'd better head home."

Callie couldn't allow them to part on such an awkward note. All through dinner, she'd felt a connection growing stronger and stronger between them. She didn't want it to break just because the evening was coming to an end.

Standing, she reached for his hand and pressed it tightly between hers. The contact brought his eyes down to hers and, in that moment, Callie felt something deep and real stir inside her.

Oh Lord, she couldn't fall for this man. He still loved his late wife. He had a child to remind him of the woman every day. The warnings zinged through her mind, yet as Callie looked up at his handsome face, none of them seemed to matter.

"This night has been so special for me, Tyler. I'd like very much for you to kiss me good-night. But if you're not ready for that kind of closeness, I'll understand."

His brows shot up and then, with a frustrated shake of his head, curled his hands over her shoulders and pulled her into his arms. When his mouth fastened over hers, Callie's knees threatened to buckle and she instinctively grabbed the front of his shirt to brace herself.

His lips roamed hers in a gentle yet devouring way and before she could actually register what was happening, her senses spun off into the starlit sky. For long, heated seconds all she could do was stand motionless and drink in the heady sensations of his masculine taste, and the warm clamp of his fingers sinking into the flesh of her shoulders.

Sparks of light showered behind her closed eyelids, while heat plunged from her face all the way to her feet. She was going to combust into a flame right here in his arms.

The wild thought was racing through Callie's mind when suddenly he lifted his head and stepped back from her.

"Good night, Callie."

Before she could utter any sort of reply, he walked off toward his truck and left Callie to stare after him in stunned silence.

Good night, Callie. That was all he'd had to say after the kiss they'd just shared?

Her lips were on fire and she was breathing as though she'd just climbed several flights of stairs. Hadn't he experienced the same earth-shaking reaction? She'd thought so.

But his lips could've been acting out of sync, she mentally argued with herself. He might have been kissing Callie while his mind had been on the late Mrs. Abernathy.

No! She wasn't going to let her thoughts go off in that miserable direction. Tyler had kissed *her*—Callie Sheldrick. And there had been real feeling behind it. She had to believe this was a genuine beginning for them.

"Callie, do you know if we'll be getting any more of those little skeletons holding up signs with the Bronco Ghost Tours' logo? Mrs. Landry would like to purchase a few for Halloween decorations. But she's leaving town tomorrow and won't be back through Bronco Heights until the first part of the year."

Callie pulled her attention away from the monitor on her desk to see Saundra standing in the open doorway that led into the booking office and gift shop.

"I'm not sure about the skeletons. I do know that Evan ordered the little ghosts and jack-o'-lanterns. If she wants them that badly, get her address and phone number. We might be able to order the skeletons and mail them to her."

"Okay, will do. And if you can spare a minute, there are customers waiting to book tours and purchase gifts."

Callie pushed herself to her feet and walked over to Saundra. "Sure. I'll do the booking if you can handle the shoppers."

Saundra's eyes narrowed on Callie's face. "Honey, are you okay? You look beat, and it's only ten o'clock in the morning!"

Callie bit back a sigh. Last night, when Tyler had left her at the bench in the courtyard and driven away, it had only been a few minutes past ten. Plenty early enough for her to get a good night's sleep. But once she'd gone inside her apartment, she'd been unable to think of getting ready for bed or going to sleep. Instead, she'd stared at the walls, thinking about Tyler's kiss and what, if anything, it had meant to him.

As for what it had meant to Callie, her head was still swimming among the clouds. Though she knew she was probably being a fool, she couldn't stop thinking about the man.

"I think I've been staring at the screen too long. I just need to rest my eyes."

Saundra hardly looked convinced. "If that's the case, maybe you should make a visit to the optometrist. You might need glasses."

A visit to the psychiatrist would probably be more in line, Callie thought. To help her regain the common sense she'd lost last night when Tyler had kissed her.

"Let's go," Callie told her. "We have customers waiting."

Out in the booking room, Callie met with a set of middle-aged parents and their two, clearly bored, teenage daughters. The man and wife were eager to take a tour, but the girls were making it clear with eye rolls and folded arms that they wanted to be anywhere but on a ghost tour.

"Our most popular tour is the downtown walking tour," Callie said to the husband and wife. "It includes a visit to the courthouse, the cemetery, and then a walk over the old train bridge to Easterbrook House."

"And how long does this tour take?" the husband inquired. "We want to get our money's worth."

"About ninety minutes," Callie answered.

"Ninety minutes!" one of the girls exclaimed. "I can't walk that long!"

With a wry shake of his head, the father turned to his daughter. "Then how do you manage to walk around the mall for two or three hours?"

"But ninety minutes is a long time, Dad," the younger looking of the two girls complained. "And it will be hot outside!"

Seeing trouble brewing, Callie attempted to reassure her. "I promise the guide will be happy to let you rest whenever you need to."

"That's because he's probably so ancient he walks with a cane," the older girl mumbled crossly. "This whole thing is stupid."

Callie wasn't so old that she'd forgotten what it was like to be a teenager being forced to accompany her parents on trips. Still, that was no cause for these girls to behave rudely.

"Sorry to disappoint you," Callie told the girl in the sweetest voice she could muster. "Josh is a young college student. But if you'd rather have a different guide, I'm sure he'd be glad to exchange tours with someone else."

The sulky demeanor on the girl's face instantly vanished. "A college guy will be guiding us? Oh! He'll be fine."

"Sure, Lacey," her sister mockingly chided her sister. "Now you're happy. But what about me? I'm going to be bored out of my mind! Dad—"

"Girls, that's enough!" the man snapped.

Even if Callie had gotten a full night's sleep, this family would still be wearing her patience paper-thin. As it was, she wished she'd chosen to assist the customers buying gifts instead of booking a tour.

"Maybe you'll have some real excitement and spot John Easterbrook's ghost," Callie told the family. "Most people around Bronco say he never left his house, even after he died. Or you might hear the gallows creaking outside the courthouse where the public executions used to take place."

Thankfully, that was enough to get the girls talking excitedly between themselves and to give the parents a chance to finish booking the tour. By the time the four of them trooped out the entrance, Callie went over to a couch supplied for waiting customers and practically fell onto the end cushion.

Now that the room was empty, Saundra

walked over to the glass door and peered out at the family moving on down the sidewalk.

"Whew. I'm glad I didn't have to deal with them! Are they actually coming back?" she asked.

"Yes. For the eight o'clock tour tonight. I only hope Josh doesn't have any problem with those girls. Maybe I'd better warn him."

"I wouldn't say anything. He's young. Josh is used to that kind of behavior."

Callie grimaced. "No matter their age. Those girls need lessons in manners."

"Tell me about it. I imagine they've been spoiled since the day they were born."

Saundra's comment caused Callie's thoughts to turn to Maeve. At this point in the baby's life, Tyler was simply trying to meet his daughter's physical and emotional needs. But later, when she was able to talk and voice her opinions, to ask for things that were out of reach, or to do things that were out of bounds, how would he handle her? Would the fact that she had no mother sway his better judgment and pressure him to give in and spoil her?

Or would he guide her with a firm but loving hand?

Callie, you need to get a grip! One kiss from Tyler and you're in a silly dreamworld. Picturing him as your husband and Maeve as your child. Do you know what a fool looks like? If you don't, then go find a mirror.

"Earth to Mars! Can you hear me, Callie? Or have we lost radio transmission?"

Saundra's voice managed to penetrate the words of warning in Callie's head and she looked blankly at her coworker.

"Sorry, Saundra. You were saying something to me?"

Saundra waved a dismissive hand through the air. "Nothing important. I was just saying we should mention to Evan about the skeletons that Mrs. Landry ordered. He'll probably want to have them restocked in the gift shop by Halloween."

"Good idea. I'll make a note." Callie forced herself up from the couch. She was about to leave the room when the door to the office opened and Vanessa Cruise stepped inside.

"Well, look at this. We're graced by royalty this morning," Saundra affectionately teased. "It's Miss Bronco in all her glory. Where's your tiara?"

Laughing, Vanessa touched a hand to the top of her head. "Don't tell me it's missing! And the one I put on this morning had the ten-carat diamond in the center."

"Don't worry," Saundra assured her. "You'll soon be wearing a ten-carat diamond on your finger."

"Don't be so sure about that." Vanessa walked over to the display window and peered at the array of the latest gifts Callie and Saundra had added to the mix.

"About what?" Callie asked. "The ten carats? Or getting engaged?"

"Callie, you've had some sort of mental breakdown this morning," Saundra chided. "You know as well as anybody that Jameson will be slipping a ring on Van's finger any day now."

"Well, she just said don't be so sure," Callie pointed out.

Vanessa's expression was something between smug and sly as she looked at both women.

"If, or when, Jameson puts a ring on my finger, I wouldn't want a rock that huge. I'd have to hire a security guard to follow me around," she joked.

"So the romance is still on?" Saundra asked.

Vanessa smiled dreamily as Callie said, "There was never any doubt about that, Saundra. Van isn't about to let Jameson get away."

Strolling over to the desk, Vanessa took a seat in one of the heavy wooden chairs positioned in front of it.

"You two are probably wondering what I'm doing in town instead of at Happy Hearts," she said.

"Well," Callie said, "it isn't exactly like you to be in town in the middle of the morning. Who's watching over your camp kids out at the animal sanctuary?"

She said, "Daphne needed a few supplies for the farm and I offered to make the trip into town to pick them up for her. She's watching the kids until I get back, so I can't dally long. I mainly stopped by to see you, Callie."

"Me? I assumed you were here to see Evan."

Shaking her head, Vanessa smiled coyly at her roommate. "I don't need to see my brother for anything. You were already in bed last night when I got home. I wanted to hear how your date with Tyler went."

From the corner of her eye, Callie could see Saundra's mouth fall open and then she scowled. "A date with Tyler! Why haven't I heard about this?" Saundra demanded. "What am I around here, anyway? Just a fixture?"

Callie shot Vanessa a censoring look before she turned to Saundra. "Sorry, Saundra. I was going to tell you about it later. And as for you, Van, how did you learn that I had a date? I haven't told anyone yet."

"Callie, it's not like an Abernathy can avoid being noticed in this town. A couple of little birdies I'm acquainted with saw you at DJ's Deluxe last night. And from every-thing they told me, it sounded like you two were getting cozy with each other."

Groaning, Callie crossed the room and re-turned to her seat on the couch. "Cozy is a total exaggeration. We were simply having dinner and a little wine. The evening was very nice and Tyler was a perfect gentleman. That's really all there was to it."

This time it was Saundra who let out a loud groan. "Oh, come on, Callie. Can't you give us one juicy detail?"

The kiss Tyler had given her was too pri-vate and special to ever share with anyone. Besides, it would probably be the one and only time she would be that close to the sexy cowboy.

"We talked—a lot," Callie admitted.

"And?" Vanessa pressed her. "Are you going to see him again?"

Callie wished she could give her friends a cool and casual response, but she figured she looked like a deer caught in the headlights. "I have no idea."

Saundra rushed over to the couch and sank next to her.

"No idea? Callie, that's ridiculous! It looks pretty obvious to me. If he took you to dinner at DJ's, he wasn't just playing around. He's interested."

"I agree with Saundra." Vanessa spoke up, then with a thoughtful frown added, "Although, most everyone I've heard speak about the guy seems to think he has a big hang-up over losing his wife."

"That's understandable," Saundra said.

Callie glanced at both women. "He does," she said flatly. "Have a hang-up about her."

A clever smile replaced Vanessa's thoughtful frown. "You know what that means, don't you?"

Callie tried not to sound defeated. "That I don't have the tiniest chance of having a meaningful relationship with the man."

"No, silly! It means you're going to have to get him over her."

Saundra's head bobbed up and down in agreement. "Van's right. If he keeps living with her memory, then he'll never really see you. And that would be a shame. He's young. His life is just starting. He needs to find love again."

Rather than let her friends see the doubtful shadows in her eyes, Callie stared at a piece of fuzz on the floor. "Listen, you two, just because my job entails ghosts, that doesn't mean I can compete with one. Especially for a man's love. No. I'm beginning to think I might be going down the wrong path. I should be regarding Tyler as a friend. Nothing more."

The signal is strong.

As Winona Cobbs's words echoed in her mind, Callie glanced past the gift shop to an alcove where a purple door painted with silver stars served as an entrance to Winona's place of business. Over the door, a tinsel-edged sign with the words *Wisdom by Winona* hung from a yellow crescent moon.

Since Evan had insisted Winona move her physic business from an outside shanty to inside the Ghost Tour building, Callie had only peeked beyond the outlandish door to the waiting room. Like the door, it was also painted entirely in purple with velvet curtains of the same color draped from the center of the ceiling to the tops of the walls. The space gave off an eerie vibe and Callie could only imagine how fantastic the actual reading area looked.

The old woman had no idea what was going on in Callie's or Tyler's life, she thought. And that comment she'd made about the signal was just as weird now as it had been at Melanie's bridal shower.

So why did the silly phrase keep running through Callie's mind?

Vanessa arched a brow at Callie. "Why are you staring at Winona's door? Are you considering asking her for romantic advice?"

Callie groaned. "Are you trying to be funny?"

Vanessa frowned while Saundra's attention vacillated between the two women.

"How could you ask that, Callie? Winona is my and Evan's great-grandmother," Vanessa reminded her. "Yes, she might seem a little quirky, but there's a keenness about her that most people don't bother to notice. And I'm not talking about her rambling predictions. I believe she understands things about us that we don't recognize in ourselves."

"Van, I don't mean to sound critical of your relatives. God knows, none of us is perfect," Callie said. "But Winona is ninety-four years old. Everything she's ever known about romance, she's surely forgotten."

"You're wrong about that, Callie. When Winona learned that Grandmother Daisy was actually Beatrix, her and Josiah's secret love child, it was like a light turned on inside her. When she talks about Josiah, love radiates from her eyes. She's not forgotten. Nor has she ever quit loving him. Winona is one of the reasons I made the decision not to settle for anything less than the real deal. A man who truly loves me. One who will be with me to the end of our lives."

"Van has a point there," Saundra told Callie, glancing impatiently at the ringing phone on the booking desk. "I'll answer it."

After she left, Callie pinched the bridge of her nose. "Van, to be honest, Tyler is… He made me feel like a princess last night. Just being with him makes me giddy. But there are times I get the feeling that he's only partially with me."

"Hmm. And you're thinking his mind is on his late wife."

"What else?" Callie asked glumly.

"Has he talked to you about her?"

"No. And that's another thing I find unsettling. You'd think he would at least say her name, or mention her offhandedly when he talks about Maeve. But he doesn't. It's like she's a giant shadow in the corner of the room that we're both trying to ignore." She let out a resigned sigh. "But I keep telling myself it's too soon. It probably hurts him too much to talk about her to anyone."

Vanessa grimaced. "If that's the case, he doesn't need to be dating. It's not fair to you."

"Well, like I said, I'm not sure we'll see each other again anyway. He didn't mention it and I didn't have an opportunity to suggest it."

No, you were too busy suggesting he kiss you good-night.

The taunting voice in her head very nearly caused her to blush, but thankfully she managed to keep the embarrassing sting from her cheeks.

Rising from the chair, Vanessa walked over to Callie and gently patted her shoulder. "You shouldn't be looking this miserable, Callie. When I walked in, I thought I'd find you walking on air. Instead, you look like you want to run off somewhere and cry for hours."

Callie did her best to smile. "I am happy, Van. I only wish I had met Tyler under different circumstances—without the tragedy of his wife's accident standing between us. Doesn't matter. I don't expect to hear from him. Not anytime soon, for sure."

"Well, as long as you don't fret over the

situation, that's the important thing. Now, I'd better get back to Happy Hearts before Daphne has the law out looking for me."

Callie rose and Van smacked a kiss on her cheek. "'Bye, sweetie. See you tonight."

"Oh, you're going to be at the apartment tonight?" Callie asked her.

Nodding, Vanessa started for the door. "Jameson is going to be busy tonight. Hey, maybe we should make a pizza or do delivery? How does that sound?"

"Wonderful."

Vanessa waved goodbye and slipped out the door.

Callie walked back to the small nook she used as her personal office. She'd just taken a seat at her desk when her cell phone pinged with an incoming text message.

Plucking up the device, she frowned at the unfamiliar number.

Who was that? Had someone accidently sent a text to her number?

She punched open the message and immediately let out a gasp of surprise.

Tyler!

Maeve and I plan to drive in to town tomorrow night for a burger. Would you like to go with us?

Suddenly it didn't matter if half of his mind was on his dead wife. Or if his feelings for Callie were little more than casual friendship. All that mattered was that he wanted to be with her.

She quickly typed out a response.

I'd love to go. What time?

Six. See you then.

Yes. Tomorrow night.

Callie put down the phone but she didn't immediately turn her focus back to the spreadsheet on the monitor. Instead, she pulled a mirror from her handbag, flipped it open and peered at her image.

The smile on her face was so wide it was about to crack the corners of her lips and her brown eyes were twinkling in a way she'd never seen before.

Was she actually looking at a fool? Or a woman who was falling in love?

Chapter Five

Because the dirt road to Tyler's house was on private Flying A land, it wasn't maintained by the county. The Abernathys had to do their own upkeep with a tractor and box blade. A job that was usually put last on the list of ranch chores. Maeve always giggled when then truck bounced over the washboard ridges and this evening was no exception as Tyler drove the narrow road that would take them off the ranch and to the nearest highway.

On the back seat, where he'd buckled the baby in her safety carrier, Maeve giggled loudly and kicked her feet with happy excitement.

"I'm glad you're enjoying this ride, sweetie," Tyler said to her. "But it won't be so funny if we end up having a flat."

He'd barely gotten the words out of his mouth when he rounded a bend and spotted Dean's truck coming toward him.

With hardly enough room for two vehicles to pass, Tyler steered his pickup off the edge of the road and braked it to a halt. His brother stopped alongside him and lowered the driver's window. Tyler did the same.

"What's up?" Tyler asked. "Are you going to my house?"

"I was. Looks like I should've called first. You going over to Mom and Dad's?"

Normally, Dean's assumption would've been correct. After Luanne died, Tyler had narrowed his travels to his parents' house, to Dean's place, or to town for supplies whenever necessary.

A sense of family duty had been the only reason he'd gone to Gabe's bachelor party and subsequently the Ambling A, where he'd first met Callie. Since then, his routine had been broken, along with his ability to focus on anything for more than two or three minutes at a time.

"Maeve and I are going to town. To have a burger," he told Dean.

"In case you've forgotten, Maeve is nine months old. She can't eat a hamburger," Dean pointed out. "She only has one tooth!"

Tyler let out a short laugh. "It's good you know that much about babies, brother. You might have one of your own someday. But to ease your worries, I'll be eating the burger. Maeve will have puréed green beans and carrots. And ice cream for a treat."

Dean chuckled. "A rancher with a freezer full of beef and he has to drive all the way to town for a hamburger. That's pretty good, Tyler."

"Sometimes a man doesn't want to cook for himself."

Chuckling again, Dean said, "Just kidding, brother. I'm thrilled you're going to be out among people. I hope this means you've decided to quit being a recluse."

Tyler had never thought of himself as a recluse. He wasn't like the hermit who used to live on a small piece of property not far from the Flying A. On rare occasions, they would spot him out of the house. His hair and beard had always been long and scraggily, his clothes little more than rags. He'd been a man who'd quit caring. Tyler hadn't quit caring. He'd just not had the energy or the heart to start his life over.

"I'll go ahead and make you a little more thrilled and tell you that I'm picking up a young lady to go with us."

Dean's jaw dropped. "Is this some of your dark humor?"

"No. I'm serious. Didn't Mom or Dad tell you I had a date the other night?"

Dean's brow furrowed. "No. And you didn't, either."

"I haven't had time. I've been hauling the last of the round bales into the ranch yard. Two hundred and fifty of them, to be exact.

I've not exactly been twiddling my thumbs or sitting around chatting."

"Who is this mystery lady?"

"Not any mystery about it. I met her at Mel's shower. You called her the 'little brunette.'"

Dean suddenly grinned. "Oh…her. That's cool, baby brother. You're venturing out and with a woman, too. A cute one, at that. This is better news than a hike in cattle prices!"

Cute. Yes, Callie was cute—and sweet and tender and all the things he'd ever wanted in a woman. Too bad Luanne had lost all those qualities after she'd married him and moved onto the Flying A, he thought ruefully.

"Thanks, brother. Uh, were you going to the house for a reason?"

"No big deal. I thought we'd sit outside for a few minutes, have a beer and listen to the crickets. But that's okay. You have more important things to do tonight." He gave Tyler a thumbs-up before he pulled his truck forward. "Get out of here. I'll see you tomorrow."

Tyler returned his brother's gesture then pulled back onto the road.

In front of him, the evening sun was beginning to take on a golden-pink hue as it spread across the wide, western horizon. To his right, green, grassy slopes swept away to low foothills that climbed up to high mountains covered with evergreen forests, jagged rocks and tumbling waterfalls. To the left, open grassland was dotted with herds of Black Angus cattle.

The beauty of the Flying A never failed to stir his emotions and fill him with pride. Some would say his deep connection to the ranch was more like an addiction. But to Tyler, the land and the cattle were more like his lifeblood. And if he was ever brave enough to invite another woman into his life, he'd make damned sure she could handle his hardworking, country life.

When he reached the juncture of graveled road and paved highway, he steered the truck toward Bronco, his thoughts taking a turn of their own, straight back to Callie. He'd been shocked when she'd suggested that he kiss her good-night. Sure, the idea of kissing her had entered his mind plenty of times. Like each time his eyes had landed on her soft, plump lips.

When the two of them had been sitting on the bench in the courtyard, the urge to kiss her, to hold her in his arms and to feel her womanly curves pressed against him had practically consumed his brain. It had been a struggle to concentrate on anything she'd been saying. Until she'd uttered those two, little words—*kiss me.*

He'd been so shaken by the intimate contact that all he'd been able to do was say goodbye and walk away. And since then, the taste of her mouth had haunted him. He wasn't supposed to want a woman like that. Not that much. Not with Luanne only being gone for a half a year. What was the matter with him, anyway?

He was lonely, he thought. And if he could be truly honest with himself, he'd been lonely long before Luanne had died.

Callie filled some of that empty ache inside him and he couldn't give that up. Not when he was just now beginning to feel like a man again.

The dining area of Bronco Burgers, the small burger place in Bronco Valley, was crowded with people stopping off for a quick meal after work. But Callie didn't notice the loud conversations or shrieking kids racing back and forth between the dining tables and the order counter. She was too busy trying to smother her laughter as she watched another spoonful of puréed green beans ooze out of Maeve's puckered lips.

"Poor little thing. I'd be spitting out that stuff, too. She wants an onion ring with ketchup," Callie told Tyler as he attempted to get his daughter to accept a bite of carrots from the baby food jar.

Chuckling, he looked over at her. "Who wouldn't? But she needs the proper vitamins. Besides, she's not old enough to digest that kind of food."

"I know. But I feel sorry for her. She sees us eating good stuff and probably wonders why she's being tortured."

"At least she's not crying," he said. "And if I can get a bit more down her, I'll let her have ice cream."

Maeve was being adorable tonight. She'd even allowed Callie to talk to her without dissolving into a mess of tears. Callie was surprised at how quickly she was taking to the baby. She'd always been so nervous around them, but the more she was around Maeve, the more comfortable she felt.

"Would you mind if I tried to feed her?" Callie asked. "If she cries, I'll give the spoon back to you."

Tyler shot her a wry grin. "Oh sure. Get her to cry, then expect me to take over."

"How will I ever learn to be a mommy if I don't start somewhere?" she asked.

Both his brows quirked and it suddenly dawned on Callie how presumptuous and suggestive she'd sounded.

"Oh, I, uh… That didn't come out right,"

she stuttered as her cheeks flamed with embarrassed heat. "I didn't mean to be, uh, a mommy to Maeve. I only meant in general terms."

He chuckled and relief poured through her.

"Don't be silly, Callie. I never thought you were trying to give me a hint."

She blew out a long breath then let out a short, self-incriminating laugh. "See, I told you I was constantly putting my foot in my mouth. My sister used to accuse me of being a rattlebrain, that I didn't think before I spoke. But it's more like I use all the wrong words."

Smiling, Tyler handed Maeve's spoon over to her. "Here. Give it a try. I think she likes the carrots better."

With the spoon balanced tightly between her fingers, Callie looked at the jars of baby food and then at Maeve. The baby was watching her with curious blue eyes, as though she didn't know what to expect next.

"Okay, Maeve," Callie said in a soft, coaxing voice. "Will you be a good girl and take a bite for me?"

Callie dipped up a bit of the mushy orange food and drew it near Maeve's lips. To her utter surprise and delight, the baby opened her mouth and allowed Callie to tip in the spoonful of carrots.

"Oh, yummy, yummy," she crooned to the baby. "And you're such a good girl."

"I'm in shock," Tyler murmured more to himself than Callie.

Slanting him a hopeful glance, she said, "I think this might work. You go ahead and enjoy your meal while I have baby training 101."

"Good luck," he said with an amused grin. "You're a brave girl. That's all I can say."

He picked up what was left of his hamburger and began to eat. Callie offered another spoonful to Maeve. The baby didn't hesitate to open her mouth and accept the food. By the third spoonful, Maeve decided it was a fun experience to have Callie feed her. Between mouthfuls, she made happy sounds, kicked her feet, and joyfully slapped her hands on the high chair tray.

Callie couldn't help but laugh at Maeve's antics and, the more she fed her, the more lost she became in the playful interaction. Before she realized how much time had passed, the spoon hit the bottom of the jar.

She glanced questioningly over at Tyler, "Have I given her enough? I don't know how much a baby eats."

His gaze slipped over her face as though he was seeing her in a different light. And perhaps he was, Callie thought. Being with him and Maeve was definitely making her feel like some other woman. Not the shy Callie who was often unsure of herself.

"That's plenty, Callie. You did great."

His compliment shouldn't make her feel like she was sitting on top of the world, but it did.

"I don't know about being great. But I'm making progress. I must not look as scary to Maeve now as I did at the bridal shower."

"That night she was tired and needed sleep."

Callie picked up a napkin and carefully wiped the last of the carrots from Maeve's face before she turned her attention to the last half of her burger.

"To tell you the truth, Tyler, I was bored out of my mind. I yawned so many times, Vanessa scolded me."

"I was bored, too," he said with a guilty grin.

"Well, you had a right to be. You're a man," she reasoned. "Women are supposed to get excited over kitchen appliances and fancy linens. I couldn't work myself up over any of it."

She couldn't explain to Tyler that her lack of excitement stemmed from having no man in her life. Or no plans for a family of her own. It was too embarrassing.

"I'm glad we were both there," he said. "And that Erica introduced you to me."

His remark put a detour on her dark musings. Perhaps he did like her company. But that didn't mean she should allow her burgeoning feelings for Tyler to get out of hand. For both of their sakes, she needed to slow down and give him the time he needed to get accustomed to being with a woman again.

"I'm glad, too," she murmured and then turned a smile on Maeve. "And Maeve will be happy when she gets ice cream."

Feigning a weary sigh, he stood. "Ice cream coming up. Would you like some, too? Dipped in chocolate?"

Chuckling, she said, "You've been gazing into Winona's crystal ball again."

Amused, he arched a brow at her. "Does she have a crystal ball in her fortune shop?"

"I've never gone into Winona's shop. But I have a feeling if she does have a crystal ball, I'd probably gaze in it and see your face."

He shot her a wry smile. "You just might, at that."

By the time they returned to Callie's apartment complex, Maeve's little head listed to one side of the safety seat and drool oozed from the corner of her parted lips.

"I was going to ask you in for coffee, but you probably don't want to wake her," Callie said.

If Tyler had any sense, he'd go straight home, put Maeve in her crib and call it a night. But what would that accomplish? He'd end up staring at the walls and wishing he'd stayed here with Callie.

"I doubt she'll wake up if I carried her inside," he said. "Her tummy is full and she hasn't had a nap in hours."

Callie looked at him and the eager little smile on her face was impossible for Tyler to resist.

"Then you'd like to come in?" she asked. "I have a whole box of pastries left over from the office today. You need to eat them before I do."

He chuckled. "I see. You need me for a food disposal. Okay, I'd like to come in— for a few minutes."

"Great. I'll go unlock the door and turn on the lights while you get Maeve," she told him.

A couple of minutes later, he carried the sleeping baby into the apartment. As he surveyed the living room in search of a safe place to lay her, Callie said, "I wish we had a crib to put her in, but the armchair might be large enough to hold her."

"That ought to work. As long as she doesn't decide to roll."

Callie glanced around for a solution. "We can push the footstool against the front of the chair," she suggested. "That way Maeve would have to roll several times before she hit the floor."

"Good idea." He placed Maeve in the chair and, after pushing the stool into place, stepped aside to let Callie cover the baby with a soft afghan.

"She looks pretty comfy." She straightened to her full height and turned to face him. "Why don't you have a seat and I'll bring the coffee and pastries in here. That way you can keep an eye on her."

She was standing less than an arm's length away. Close enough for him to smell the scent of flowers on her skin, to see the amber flecks in her brown eyes, and the faint lines in her lips. Those oh so soft lips.

Drawing in a deep breath, he shoved mightily at the urge to grab her and kiss her until neither one of them could breathe.

"Uh, thanks," he managed to say. "I'll… um…do that if you can manage in the kitchen."

"I can't cook, but I can make coffee," she said wryly. "Make yourself comfortable and I'll be right back."

After she left the room, Tyler took a seat on the couch. The picture window was directly in front of him and beneath the glow of the lamps situated around the U-shaped courtyard, he could make out the image of the tree and the bench beneath the drooping limbs. Even if he lived to be an old man, he knew he'd always remember how it had felt to have Callie's lips softly yielding to his.

"Here it is," she said quietly as she entered the living room carrying a red plastic tray loaded with cups and a plate of pastries. "I brought cream and sugar, too. I noticed the other night at DJ's that you drank it that way."

From the moment Tyler had picked her up this evening, he'd been charmed by how cute she looked in skinny blue jeans and a pink T-shirt that hugged her upper body. Now as she placed the tray on the coffee table and sat next to him, he couldn't help but notice the way her rounded breasts strained against the jersey top and how the faded denim outlined her thighs.

Drawing in a deep breath, he forced his eyes onto the tray. "My brothers call me a wimp for drinking it that way. But their teasing doesn't bother me. My mom's dad, Abel McEntire, always took his coffee with cream and sugar and he was a mountain of a man."

"Is he still living?"

He shook his head. "No. Grandad Abel passed about three years ago. He was a coal miner for most of his life and a Viet Nam veteran. He received a Purple Heart, but he hardly ever talked about his service in the army. I always made a point to tell him how proud I was of him. Not only for his service to our country but because he was a good man all around."

She handed him one of the coffees and a spoon.

"Hearing such admiration from his grandson must have made him feel good," she said.

"Actually, whenever I bragged on him, it always brought tears to his eyes. Even though he was a big, tough man on the outside, on the inside he was a marshmallow."

Stirring the cream and sugar into his cup, he thought about the past three years of his life. He'd gained a beautiful little daughter. But he'd lost his Granddad Abel and Luanne. And throughout it all, Tyler had continued to push himself forward for Maeve's sake. He'd promised himself that the passing of time would dim the grief and the memories. But so far he was still waiting.

Her brown eyes met his and she smiled

ever so gently. "Then if I were you, I'd be proud to drink my coffee like him."

Outside of their compatibility in the bedroom, Luanne had never understood what made Tyler tick. How was it that Callie seemed to recognize what was important to him and brush aside the things that weren't? He'd never had a girlfriend exactly like her. To be honest, it was a bit unsettling to admit she could be that in sync with him.

His thoughts, plus the quietness of the apartment left him feeling restless. In an effort to relieve it, he leaned forward and took a glazed bismark from the stack of pastries. "Vanessa isn't home tonight?" he asked.

Callie squared around on the cushion so that she was facing him and rested her shoulder against the back of the couch. "No. She's out at Jameson's ranch."

"I imagine you miss her," he said.

A wan smile touched her face. "You can tell?"

"I can hear it in your voice—like you've lost your best friend," he explained.

"Oh. Well, I haven't exactly lost Van. She'll always be one of my very best friends. But she'll be moving out soon and..." She paused and blew out a heavy breath. "You'll probably think this is funny, but I have to admit that it's been kinda hard on me seeing all my friends getting engaged and married. They're all moving on and starting new lives. I'm still wondering if I'll ever find the right man for me."

The odd little pain he heard in her voice made him wonder if she'd really loved her ex and just hadn't wanted to admit it to Tyler. He hoped not. He hated to think of any man breaking her heart and tossing aside her dreams.

"I don't think that's funny, Callie."

"Thanks," she said, then smiled and asked, "You knew that Winona Cobbs is Vanessa's great-grandmother, didn't you?"

"I overheard my parents discussing it one evening when all of us brothers were having dinner with them. Mom said that most of the folks around Bronco were shocked when they learned that Winona had had a secret affair with Josiah Abernathy."

"Not only that, she had his baby and the Abernathys told Winona the child was still-born! Poor woman, it's no wonder she had to be institutionalized from a mental break-down. None of that would've happened if the Abernathys hadn't slunk out of town dur-ing the night and taken the baby with them. They didn't even have the decency to keep the baby for Josiah's sake. They adopted her out."

"I hope you're not lumping that set of Ab-ernathys with my branch of the family."

"Oh, not at all," she assured him. "It's ob-vious your family is nothing like Josiah's was back then."

"I can tell you that my parents were both stunned when they heard the story," Tyler told her. "Why did you ask about Winona anyway?"

"Yesterday, Van told me and my coworker that Winona had more or less opened her eyes to what she wanted for herself and the future."

Tyler was dumbfounded. "Don't tell me that Vanessa had the old woman read her palm or gaze into that crystal ball we were talking about."

Callie smiled and shook her head. "No. Van isn't that mystical. She only meant that learning about Winona and Josiah's love affair showed her that real love continues on—in spite of years of separation. Van decided that she wouldn't settle for anything less than the deep kind of love her great-grandmother experienced. And, honestly, I want that same thing. I'm just not sure I'll ever be lucky enough to find it."

Yes, Tyler could understand Callie wanting to be a wife and mother. But right now, he didn't want to think about her walking down the aisle with Mr. Right. He wanted to think about this very moment and how it felt to have her close to him, even if it was just to talk, to smile at him and to make him feel as though he was a better man than the one who'd caused his wife to die.

She was doing it again, Callie thought. Putting her foot in her mouth and talking about things that were making Tyler uncomfortable. No wonder there was a frown creasing the space between his brows.

She hadn't purposely guided their conversation to the subject of love and marriage. His question about Vanessa had done that. But she should've had more forethought than to bring up Winona and Josiah's love affair and how it had lasted all these decades. But it was too late to take it back. Now the only thing she could do was to steer their conversation to something mundane and safe. Like the weather. Or the price of cattle. Surely ranchers liked to discuss those subjects.

Callie glanced over at him with the intention of asking him about the cattle market, but when she saw him licking the crumbly glaze from the bismark off his fingers, she instantly forgot the question and jumped to her feet.

"Sorry, Tyler. I forgot to bring napkins for the pastries. I'll be right back."

He shook his head. "I don't need a napkin."

"Yes—yes, you do."

She hurried around to the kitchen nook and with trembling fingers snatched several napkins from a holder on the counter. But instead of going directly back to join Tyler on the couch, she braced her weight against the cabinet and pressed a palm to her heated forehead.

She had to get a grip. Just because Tyler was in the apartment, sitting on her couch and looking like a sexy maverick in boots and jeans, didn't mean she had to suffer a meltdown! It didn't mean she had to rattle nervously on about things he probably considered as annoying as fingernails scraping over a blackboard.

"Callie, is anything wrong?"

Dropping her hand, she saw Tyler walking

toward her. A frown of real concern was on his face.

Oh Lord, now she was going to turn pink with embarrassment, she thought. He must be thinking she was the most immature twenty-five-year-old he'd ever met. And at this very moment, she'd have to agree with him.

"I, uh, I'm fine," she said shakily. "I was just catching my breath."

"Are you feeling light-headed? I'll help you back to the couch."

Callie lifted her gaze to his and the urge to laugh and cry hit her at the same time. In an attempt to swallow the impulses, a strangled sound gurgled in her throat.

"I'm okay, Tyler. Really. I'm just feeling like an idiot. That's all."

"Why?"

She groaned and though she wanted to cover her face with both hands, she forced them to remain at her sides. "Because—I don't know, Tyler, something happens to me whenever I'm with you. I start talking and behaving like a fool. I'm sorry. I wouldn't blame you if you wanted to get the heck out of here."

"Why?" he asked again.

"Do you have to ask? I talk about all the wrong things and I—"

"Callie," he gently admonished, "don't."

He stepped close enough to pull her into his arms and Callie was too dazed to do anything but wrap her arms around his waist and lay her cheek against his chest.

Oh my, it felt so good to feel his solid strength next to her, the warmth of his arms holding her as though he considered her precious.

"I'm sorry," she said again, her voice muffled by his denim shirt. "I shouldn't be nervous around you, but I am. Because I—I've never felt like this before."

His thumb and forefinger lifted her chin just far enough for him to look into her eyes. "I've never felt like this before, either."

"You don't have to say that to make me feel better."

"I'm being honest."

Her heart had already been tap dancing. Now it was madly jackhammering against her breastbone.

"Then I should be honest, too," she said. "I'm afraid, Tyler. Of myself. Of what might happen."

His hand gently cupped the side of her face and Callie wondered if a person could actually melt like ice cream in the hot sun.

"Nothing is going to happen unless we both want it to happen," he murmured softly.

Maybe not physically, she thought. But what about her heart? With each minute she was with this man, she felt a little piece of it being lost to him. How much more of it could she stand to lose?

When she made no effort to reply he said, "You believe me, don't you?"

She had to believe him. The connection she felt to him was too deep to start running scared now.

Don't be afraid.

Winona's words zinged through her mind,

but just as quickly flew out of her head as she watched Tyler's lips slowly lower toward hers.

The contact set off a tiny explosion inside her and this time Callie didn't worry about who or what was on his mind. Nor did she try to tamp down her heated response to his kiss. He wanted her and she wanted him. Nothing else mattered.

As his lips probed hers, she felt his arms tightening around her, drawing her closer to the hard length of his body. He smelled like a man. Tasted like a man. And Callie couldn't get enough of him.

She was close to running out of oxygen when he finally lifted his head and she opened her eyes to see his blue eyes were half closed and clouded with desire.

"Let's go back to the couch," he whispered.

Nodding, she reached for his hand and led him out to the living room. A quick glance in Maeve's direction told her the baby was still sleeping peacefully.

Tyler's gaze followed hers and he spoke

quietly, "She isn't going to wake anytime soon."

He tugged her down on the couch and straight into his arms. Callie sighed with longing as he pressed his cheek against hers and threaded his fingers through her hair.

"This feels so good," she whispered against his ear. "To be close to you like this."

"I think I've wanted this from the first moment I saw you, Callie. I don't understand it. And maybe I shouldn't try."

She pulled her head back far enough to look at him. "No. Let's not try to analyze whatever this is. Let's just enjoy."

"Yes," he agreed. "That I can do." With both hands cradling her face, he drew her lips to his.

Callie's senses took off in a dizzying whirl as he kissed her, slowly at first, and then more deeply, until her entire body was sizzling, aching to get closer to his.

Her mind was little more than a muddle of hot desire as she curled her arms around his neck and opened her mouth to accept the gentle probe of his tongue. When it slipped past her teeth, she gloried in the taste of him and the slow, seductive inspection he made of the ribbed roof of her mouth and the sharp edges of her teeth.

When the necessity for oxygen eventually forced their mouths to part, he buried his face against the curve of her neck.

"Callie, I wasn't expecting this to happen," he said hoarsely. "For us to get—"

She finished for him. "Get a little crazy with each other?"

"Get out of hand. That's what I was going to say. Because none of what just happened with us was crazy. It was incredible." He lifted his head and looked at her. "But I think we…uh, should pull on the reins a bit. Give ourselves time to process what's happening between us."

A part of her was disappointed. Yet in the rational part of her mind that was still able to think, she understood that to rush him would certainly cause her to lose him. "You're right, Tyler. We should slow down."

He stroked his fingers through her hair and Callie realized Tyler didn't have to be kissing her to light a flame inside her. All he had to do was touch her in the simplest of ways.

"Then you understand?"

"Completely."

Frowning, he pulled back as his eyes inspected her flushed face. "You look regretful now, Callie. Are you wishing none of this had happened?"

"I'm not wishing anything of the sort. It's just that you seem to click a switch in me."

A faint smile quirked his lips and Callie very much wanted to kiss the gentle expression. She wanted to wrap her arms around him, pull him down with her onto the couch and persuade him to make love to her. But she didn't. She had to wait for him. She had to respect the fact that he needed time.

"You click two switches in me and neither one of them is the off switch."

Callie smiled back at him. "Would you like to finish your coffee? I'll pour you a fresh cup."

A soft glow appeared in his blue eyes as he touched a forefinger to the middle of her lips. "I'd rather do something else. But for now, I'll settle for the coffee."

Chapter Six

The afternoon was hot with hardly a breeze to offer any sort of relief as Tyler and his father rode their horses over rocky foothills and draws to push a small herd of Angus to a pasture on the far north side of the ranch. The little two-man cattle drive had taken nearly three hours to complete, but the open gate ahead of them was the end of the journey.

To keep the cattle moving toward their final destination, Tyler popped the bridle reins against the leg of his scarred chaps, while a few yards to his right, Hutch called out to the stragglers.

"Yip! Yip! Ho, cattle! Get along through there!"

When the last calf raced through the opening to join his mama, Tyler called over to Hutch. "You keep them back, Dad. I'll get down and shut the gate."

Hutch held up a gloved hand to acknowledge he'd heard his son's suggestion and Tyler quickly dismounted to fasten the slatted metal gate.

"It's good we managed to get this last herd moved today," Hutch said as Tyler swung himself back into the saddle. "Rain is supposed to hit by the end of the week and I don't have to tell you how many times we've had to pull stuck calves from those bogs at the foot of the draw."

"Too many times," Tyler agreed as he reined his bay horse alongside his father's gray mare and pulled the gelding to a stop. "They'll be high and dry now."

Hutch reached for a canteen hanging from

the saddle horn and unscrewed the lid. After swigging several swallows of tepid water, he said, "Yeah. We just need to keep an eye on the windmill. It's the only water supply for this pasture."

Tyler mopped the sweat from his face with a bandana, then jammed the yellow cloth into the back pocket of his jeans. "I'll do it. I like to ride out to this part of the ranch anyway."

Hutch gazed around at the foothills dotted with juniper and the grass valley sweeping to the south. "It's lonesome out here, but it's damned pretty," he mused aloud. "Your mother often used to say she wanted a house out here so that she could look out at the valley from the kitchen window. I finally convinced her that it's too far off the grid to build here. Cost a fortune to run power lines this far."

Tyler glanced over at his father's tall, imposing image. Hutch Abernathy was the epitome of a Montana rancher. Even at sixty-four, he was still a strong, vibrant man who sat the saddle better than most men half his age. Years of working outside in the elements had turned his face a leather-worn tan and etched deep lines at the corners of his eyes and mouth. Gray spattered the dark hair at his temples and the day-old whiskers on his jaws.

People that knew the family often remarked that Tyler was a younger version of his father. And he supposed they did resemble each other. But their likeness stopped with their outer appearance. If Tyler lived to be a hundred, he'd never fill Hutch Abernathy's boots.

His father had always been a devoted husband. After all these years, he was still madly in love with his wife and he'd raised five sons the right way with plenty of firmness and even more love. And through it all, he'd managed to keep the Flying A productive and profitable. Not an easy feat considering they'd gone through droughts and blizzards, market crashes and a wild fire that had destroyed a third of the ranch's grazing land.

"You look troubled, son. Is everything okay with Maeve?"

Damn. How was it that his father could read his face and pick up on his thoughts with a single glance? Compared to Hutch, Winona Cobbs was an amateur mind reader.

"She's fine. When I left her with Mom this morning, she was crawling all over the kitchen floor like a happy little bug."

Tyler couldn't tell his father the real reason for the preoccupied frown on his face. Just thinking of how much he'd wanted to make love to Callie two nights ago was enough to fill him with a confusing mixture of guilt and need.

Hutch grinned as he lowered the brim of his Stetson and squinted into the sun. "She'll be walking before long. Then you'll really have your hands full."

That particular milestone in his daughter's development was something Tyler had been thinking about a lot lately. Since Luanne's death, he'd vowed to make Maeve his first priority, and he'd kept that promise by giving the baby around-the-clock attention and care. But there were times, like today, when certain jobs on the ranch made it impossible to take the baby along.

"When Maeve starts walking, she'll run Mom ragged. I can't let that happen. I'm going to have to come up with a different solution for babysitting."

"Watching Maeve is a highlight for your mother. I figure she'd have to get mighty rowdy before she could run Hannah ragged."

Tyler shook his head. "Maeve is my responsibility. Not Mom's. Dean keeps suggesting that I hire a nanny. But hell, Dad, who could I trust? The woman would definitely need to be good with childcare, but she'd also have to be dependable enough to show up whenever she was needed. No. I don't like the idea of a stranger coming in as Maeve's nanny. And all my cousins have jobs of their own."

"Are you telling me that the worry over Maeve's childcare is what's been putting that far-off look on your face?" Hutch asked.

Tyler pushed his gray Stetson back on his head and wiped his forehead with the sleeve of his shirt. "Not exactly, Dad. I just have a bunch of things on my mind, that's all."

Beneath him, the gelding moved restlessly. As far as the horse was concerned, he'd already figured out that the job at this spot on the ranch was over and it was time to head back to the barn. But Tyler knew his father wouldn't be ready to leave until he'd had his say.

"I hear you've been seeing a young lady in town," Hutch said. "Is she causing you problems?"

Tyler stared at the middle of his saddle horn rather than meet his father's inquisitive look.

"I guess Mom told you about Callie."

"She said you took her to dinner at DJ's Deluxe the other night," Hutch told him. "And a friend of mine mentioned that he'd seen the three of you at Bronco Burgers."

"Word gets around this town awfully damned fast."

"Is it supposed to be a secret?"

"No." Tyler forced himself to look at his father. "But I hate to think how people talk. They'll be saying 'Tyler's wife is hardly cold in her grave and he's already found another woman.'"

"Are you honestly worried about what other people think? Or more concerned about what you're thinking?"

Tyler frowned. "What does that mean?"

"Just that I figure you're agonizing over the fact that you've decided to live again. To let yourself look at another woman. You feel like you're cheating on Luanne. Even though she's dead and gone."

Scowling, Tyler muttered, "That's a damned brutal way of putting it."

"You're a grown man now, son. I don't intend to play softball with you."

He absently flipped the ends of the reins back and forth across the cantle of the saddle. "Well, just think about it, Dad. If you lost Mom, how would you feel about dating again? Even marrying again?"

"I can't really say, Ty. A man can't be sure

about such things until he's actually faced with the situation," Hutch said. "Your mother and I have talked about it before. She's told me that if anything should happen to her, she wants me to marry again. And she truly means it, because you see, she loves me and wants me to be happy. And I've told her the same thing. Because I'd never want her to feel chained to my ghost. I'd want her to keep living. To love again. That's what we're put on this earth to do, son. Don't you agree?"

"Sure, I agree," Tyler conceded. "But it's different for me."

Hutch gave him a lopsided smile. "One of these days, you'll figure out it isn't different for you." He reined the gray mare to the south and the Flying A Ranch yard. "Come on. We still need to repair that stretch of fence down by the creek. Unless Dean or Garrett remembered to take care of it."

"I doubt it," Tyler said of his older brothers. "They decided to take off to the horse sale in Kalispell. Didn't they tell you?"

Hutch cursed under his breath. "I haven't

heard anything about a horse sale! Do those boys seriously think we need more horses on the Flying A? Ten of our mares will foal this coming spring. Hell, even as the count stands right now, I cringe every time I look at the feed bill."

Tyler smiled in spite of himself. "Aw, Dad, they love horses—and who's to blame for that?"

Chuckling, Hutch nudged the mare into a long trot and Tyler followed at his side.

"Okay, Ty," Hutch told him. "Let's go fix the fence and pray your brothers come home with an empty horse trailer."

The two men fell silent as they rode south from the foothills and across a prairie of green grass dotted here and there with purple sage. As they traveled, Tyler's mind revisited his father's words of advice. Hutch had meant for them to be positive, uplifting, and Tyler appreciated his effort. But even his own father hadn't known the depth of agony he'd gone through in his marriage. There'd been a point when Tyler had come to realize that Luanne hadn't loved him. And he was beginning to recognize that he might not have really loved her. At least, not in the same sense as his parents loved each other.

Now there was Callie to think about. Oh Lord, she was all he'd been thinking about. Being with her made him happy. That was simple enough to figure out. But did he have a right to be happy? And being this torn, how could he ask Callie to have any sort of relationship with him? It wouldn't be fair to her.

And yet the more he pondered about Callie, the more he realized he couldn't just stop seeing her. He couldn't go back to the dark, lonely pit he'd been living in these past six months. He could only hope that the more they were together, the more he could put the past behind him.

He looked over at his father. "Dad?"

"Yeah. I'm listening."

"When you met Mom for the first time, did you know she was the one? I'm talking about knowing deep down where it really counts."

Hutch pulled the mare into a walk as a

thoughtful smile crossed his face. "I think she hated the very sight of me. But yes, I knew. Something about her voice and the way she looked with her face all soft and pretty and her eyes like blue flames—I told myself that she was the woman I wanted to be with the rest of my life. Now, if you ask your mother, she'll probably tell you a different story. That she had to chase me around for six whole weeks before I caved in and proposed to her. It was actually four weeks, but Hannah likes to exaggerate."

Tyler only wished he'd taken four weeks before he'd persuaded Luanne to marry him. But his stay in Chicago had only been for two weeks and he had not wanted to leave the city without her. What a young, immature fool he'd been. And Luanne had paid the biggest price for his mistake.

"Ty, are you getting serious ideas about this woman?"

Glancing over at his father, Tyler did his best to give him a reassuring smile. "We've only known each other a short time. Right now, we just enjoy each other's company. And I don't want to jump into something that I might later regret."

Hutch studied him for a short moment before turning his attention to the trail they were following through a stand of sage.

"Just don't let yourself be too afraid to jump, Ty."

"You're leaving work early?" Saundra asked as she watched Callie clear the top of her desk.

"Only thirty minutes. I'm caught up on everything and, since today has been slow, Evan is okay with me taking off early."

Saundra glanced over her shoulder to make sure no one could overhear her before she said in a lower voice, "Our boss is getting soft. When you first came to work here, I'll bet you wouldn't have had the nerve to ask Evan for time off. He was going through assistants like a coyote in a chicken yard."

"That was nine months ago. And to be fair, Evan had all sorts of stressful things going on in his life. I think it would be safe to say he's much happier now."

Saundra's little grin was clever as she continued to study Callie. "Hmm. You've been looking mighty happy yourself these past few days. Guess you have something special planned? Like a long bubble bath and a glass of wine."

"Saundra, your nose is getting longer and longer. You might as well come straight out and ask me what I'm doing."

The other woman feigned a wounded look. "I'm not a busybody. Oh, okay, I confess I'm nosy as heck."

Callie pulled her handbag from a desk drawer and stood. "Since you're just dying to know, I'll tell you. I'm going with Tyler and his daughter to Happy Hearts Animal Sanctuary. And I asked for the thirty minutes so we'd have plenty of daylight to look over the animals."

Saundra tapped a calculating finger against her chin. "Let's see if I have this right. Three nights ago, Tyler took you to the pizza parlor. The next night you were back at Bronco Burgers, and last night you took sandwiches to the park. Now you're going on a trip to the country. I think I'd be safe in predicting that you're going to have a date with Tyler every night this week."

Callie grinned and shrugged. "It does look that way, doesn't it? But I expect our dates will soon slow up. He and his brothers are planning to start a big fencing project on the Flying A and they want to get it finished before autumn weather hits."

Shaking her head, Saundra followed Callie out of the office and down a narrow hallway that led to a back exit of the building. "I wouldn't bet on it. I think you've put a spell on him. Or maybe you had Winona put one on him for you," she added slyly.

Callie laughed at that idea. "No spells. We're just enjoying each other's company."

"Enjoying. Is that what you call it?" Saundra asked.

"Saundra, you have a naughty mind."

A wicked grin put a twinkle in her coworker's eyes. "Not really. I just happen to know what Tyler Abernathy looks like. He'd be darned hard to resist."

"Don't worry, dear friend. I have a will of iron." She gave Saundra a wave then quickly exited the building.

As Callie drove her Jeep through the busy streets toward her apartment complex, she had to admit that Saundra was right. Tyler was very nearly impossible to resist. But these past three nights she'd spent with him hadn't required her to summon any amount of resistance. After that one night, when their kisses had gotten out of hand, he'd only kissed her a handful of times and those had been the short, sweet kind.

Callie assumed he was keeping his distance as a way to play safe. Most likely, he needed time to adjust to the connection that had seemed to spring up between them almost instantly. Still, she could only wonder where all of this time spent together was going to lead. Would he ever be ready to take her into his arms and make love to her?

Throughout the remainder of the drive, Callie purposely pushed the question out of her mind. For now, Tyler was making it apparent that he liked being with her, and that had to be enough.

Once she reached her apartment, she hurriedly changed into a pair of bell-bottomed jeans then tucked a baby-blue tank top into the waistband. After pulling her hair into a ponytail and fastening it with a blue-and-white scrunchie to match her top, she attached a pair of silver hoops to her ears and then dabbed blusher on her cheeks.

She'd just finished swiping a bit of coral gloss onto her lips and touching a few drops of perfume to her wrists and behind her ears, when the doorbell rang.

At the front door, she glanced through the peephole and saw Tyler's tall frame standing on the small square of concrete porch. The baby was in his arms, making *da-da-do* noises while chewing on her fist. The sight of the two filled her with ridiculous joy and she wasted no time in opening the door and encompassing both father and baby in a bright smile.

"Hi, Tyler!" she greeted. "Come on in. I promise I'll be ready to go in two minutes."

"If that's the case, there's no need for me to come in. I'll take Maeve out to the bench. If we're lucky, she'll spot a squirrel."

"Fine with me," she told him. "I'll be right out."

Inside the apartment, she gathered a few things she thought she might need on their trip to Happy Hearts. Once she had them all stuffed into her shoulder bag, she carefully locked the door of the apartment behind her and walked out to the courtyard to join him and the baby.

When she reached the tree, Tyler had stood Maeve on her feet and was holding onto both her hands to keep her steady.

Callie halted a few steps from the pair and stared in wonder. "Oh my goodness, Maeve is standing! I didn't know she could do this!"

Pride etched the smile on his face. "These

last few days, she's been trying to pull up and balance herself. She still needs help, but she's getting closer to standing on her own."

He carefully walked Maeve a few steps forward until the two of them were directly in front of Callie. She quickly squatted to be closer to the baby's level.

"Hi, sweet Maeve." Callie spoke gently. "Are you ready to go see the animals?"

To Callie's surprise, the girl responded with a happy squeal and followed it up with blowing a string of bubbles.

Laughing, Callie looked eagerly up at Tyler. "Do you think she might let me hold her? I'd love to carry her to the truck. But I don't want to make her cry."

"She's been letting you feed her without a fuss. She might be ready for you to hold her. Go ahead and try."

Still squatted on her heels, Callie held her hands out to Maeve. The baby bounced and then, with a joyful shriek, attempted to take a wobbly step toward Callie.

"Oh, what an angel." Callie scooped up the baby, stood and shifted her to a comfortable position in her arms. Maeve was instantly mesmerized with Callie's face and made a quick grab for her nose.

Laughing, Callie let the baby playfully squeeze her nose before she lowered her arm. "That's a good enough inspection for now, don't you think?"

Maeve must have agreed because she didn't try for Callie's nose a second time. Instead, she grabbed for her ponytail and gave it a hard tug.

Tyler chuckled as Callie carefully extricated the strands of hair from Maeve's little fist.

"Now you've done it," he said. "She'll be wanting you to hold her all the time."

"That's the idea." She cast him a triumphant smile. "Now Daddy can rest and I'll get more baby lessons."

During the drive out to Happy Hearts Animal Sanctuary, Tyler could hardly keep his eyes off Callie and on the narrow country road.

This evening there was nothing special about her tank top or jeans, but he had to admit she looked downright sexy. With her arms and shoulders bare, and her hair pulled up off her neck, the sight of all that creamy skin had him wanting to reach over and touch her. And the idea of tasting it with his lips was enough to send a blast of desire down his spine.

Since Tyler and his father had talked on their ride to the ranch house three days ago, he'd done plenty of thinking. Hutch had encouraged him to be brave enough to reach for what he wanted. And there was no doubt that he wanted Callie in the worst kind of way.

So far, he'd managed to keep his desire for her in check. He'd purposely made their kisses brief. Yet even that simple contact with her was like playing with fire and exposing himself to temptation.

"I haven't been out to Happy Hearts in ages," Callie said as Tyler drove the truck deeper into the countryside. "This is a treat for me. And I'm sure it will be for Maeve, too."

"Maeve sees cows and horses on the ranch. And she gets to play with the barn cats and dogs. But she's never been around any other animals."

"Daphne has everything on the farm. From rabbits and goats to chickens and ducks. Pigs, cows, horses and an assortment of cats and dogs. Evan says she takes in orphaned or deserted animals as long as she has room to house them."

"What does Evan think about her running the farm? I ask because a cousin of mine implied that the sanctuary was once a bone of contention between Daphne and Evan."

"Maybe in the beginning. Daphne says Evan was a cynic when they'd first met and she showed him around the farm. According to her, he didn't care about the needy animals or her efforts to help them. He was all about making a dollar off the ghost tours of the property." She paused and sighed. "But after he fell in love with Daphne, he began to have a change of heart. If you ask him about Happy Hearts now, I'm sure he'd say he's proud of Daphne's cause and all the hard work she puts into it."

He nodded soberly. "Loving a woman can change a man."

She glanced over at him. "Yes, you would know about that."

Her assumption caused Tyler to inwardly cringe. She had no idea he'd had a troubled marriage. Hell, how could she? He couldn't even bring himself to mention Luanne's name in their conversations.

Callie deserved more from him. He recognized that much. Yet each time he'd felt the urge to tell her about the circumstances of Luanne's accident, the fear of her reaction sent a cold chill rushing over him. If she knew what a failure he'd been as a husband and father, what would she think? That she wanted no part of a man like him? He wasn't ready to take that chance.

His churning thoughts were interrupted

when she spoke again. "Did you know Bronco Ghost Tours has a Happy Hearts tour?"

Shaking his head, he shot her a look of droll disbelief. "I've heard bits of gossip about Happy Hearts being haunted, but never paid much attention to the stories. I figured most of them were made up."

"The ghost tour stories aren't made up. That would never work. Anyone could delve into Bronco's history to see whether these tragedies actually occurred. If people discovered they were fake, it would end the business!"

His short laugh was skeptical. "So Happy Hearts is truly supposed to be haunted? Oh, come on, Callie. Do you really believe that?"

"I'm sure it sounds silly to you. But there is a tragic story behind the theory. Years ago, a big barn on the property caught fire and as a result, a cowboy, his girlfriend, and several horses died in the flames. There's even a marker on the farm where the couple was buried."

"I understand that incident did actually

happen. And it was certainly unfortunate," Tyler said. "But that doesn't mean there are ghosts around the place."

"Perhaps not. But since the tragedy, some folks have heard horses whinnying at night when there were no horses on the property. And others swear they've seen the faces of a man and woman peering through the barn windows."

Tyler made a scoffing noise. "You actually believe such a thing?"

"Okay, maybe some old-timers have embellished the story to scare people. But there is an archived newspaper article about the fire and it did state that a man and woman, along with the horses, perished in the flames. As for the rest, I guess it depends on who actually heard the whinnying or saw the faces. I will say this, Evan does sort of fudge the end of the tour lecture. To please Daphne, the guests are told that since the property has been turned into a happy home for needy animals, the faces of the cowboy and his girlfriend have never been seen again."

"Okay, that does it," Tyler said jokingly. "I'm spooked. You're going to have to hold my hand the whole time we're at Happy Hearts."

She slanted him an impish smile. "I'll be glad to."

Five minutes on down the road, Happy Hearts Animal Sanctuary came into view. Situated on a gentle grassy slope with the jagged outline of mountains in the background, a big, two-story Victorian-style house stood off to the left. On the right side of the property, several yards away from Daphne's house, were a number of barns in various shapes and sizes.

As they neared the property, one road continued on past the big house, while the other veered off to the left toward a parking area designated for farm workers and visitors.

Tyler parked the truck alongside three other vehicles and, after helping Callie to the ground, fetched Maeve from her seat in the back.

Currently, a handful of adults and children were milling around the barns. Between the parking lot and the neatly maintained structures, a pair of white-and-brown goats nipped at the green grass, while a few feet away a group of ducks waddled toward the shade of a tree.

"Daphne might be in her office," Callie suggested. "It's inside the biggest barn. She also has an office in the adoption shelter. That's where she does all the paperwork for the adoptions." She pointed to another building. "That one is used for the camp kids. They come to learn about animal care and experience being on a farm. Van is probably busy counseling them right now."

"Let's go let Daphne know that we've come to visit the animals," Tyler suggested.

"Sounds good," Callie agreed.

With Tyler carrying Maeve, the three headed in the direction of the largest barn, but halfway there, Daphne emerged from a nearby utility shed. Once she spotted them, she waved and called out.

"Callie! Tyler! Wait up!"

The fresh-faced strawberry-blonde was dressed in jeans and boots and a yellow T-shirt with Save the Animals written across the front. As soon as she came within arm's reach, she grabbed Callie in a fierce hug then pulled back and encompassed all three with a wide smile.

Glancing at Tyler, Daphne confessed, "I love this woman. She single-handedly saved my fiancé's sanity."

Embarrassed by the compliment, Callie let out a good-natured groan. "Are you kidding? Evan was making it okay before I came to work as his assistant."

Laughing, Daphne shook her head and explained to Tyler. "Before Callie came along, Evan had gone through too many assistants to count. Not one of them could put up with his taskmaster attitude. But Callie is part saint or something. She was so efficient that I think Evan forgot all about snapping and snarling."

"He forgot my name, too," Callie added with a chuckle. "But he finally learned it."

Laughing, Daphne gave her another appreciative hug. "It's so good of you to come out to the farm. And what a surprise—you've brought Tyler and Maeve with you!"

"Well, actually Tyler brought me," Callie told her. "We thought Maeve would enjoy seeing the animals."

Daphne slanted Tyler a suggestive grin. "Since you don't have any animals on the ranch. Right?"

Tyler chuckled. "It's a learning experience. She's never seen farm animals like goats or pigs. And I thought you could probably use a nice donation courtesy of the Flying A."

For a moment, Daphne looked overwhelmed and Callie could understand why. Not all the ranchers in the area were keen about her decision to go vegan and save the cows. Apparently, Tyler's family had an open-minded view about the issue.

"How very nice of you, Tyler. We can use every penny we get." She looked over at Callie and winked. "I hope you realize what a thoughtful man you have here."

To have Daphne imply that Tyler was Callie's man was all it took to send a rush of heat to her cheeks. Tyler wasn't *her* man. Not by a long shot. But she supposed people around Bronco were beginning to see them out together and wondering if they were seriously a couple. Callie had been asking herself the same thing, but so far she couldn't come up with an answer. Yes, he kissed her like he meant it, but he never expressed his feelings about her in words. She could only wonder what his feelings for her were.

She darted a glance at Tyler then said, "I've noticed."

"Hey, Daphne, do you have a minute?"

Daphne glanced across the grassy yard to a young man dressed in shorts and a baseball cap. He was standing with a small group of adults and children.

"That's David, one of my high-school workers. If you two will excuse me, I'd better go to his rescue. Callie, you know your way around the farm. You and Tyler make yourself at home and stay as long as you like."

Callie waved her off. "Thanks, Daphne. No need to worry about us."

As the woman hurried away to the waiting group, Tyler admitted, "This sanctuary is another venture that I'd believed was doomed from the start."

Frowning, Callie asked, "Are all men cynical by nature?"

He shrugged. "From what I understand, the Taylors never wanted their daughter to start this farm. In fact, I think there was a big rift between her and her father over the place."

Callie nodded. "I thought Van told me the argument was over Daphne deciding to become a vegan. With her father in the beef cattle business, he believed his daughter was making laughingstocks of the Taylors."

Tyler concurred. "If you've ever met Cornelius Taylor, you'd understand. He's one of those iron-necked men who holds the notion that everyone should bend to his will."

"How ridiculous!" Callie exclaimed. "A person has a right to choose what they want to eat without being ridiculed for it."

Growing restless, Maeve turned her attention to her daddy's ear. After she'd slapped it a few times, he gently placed her hand down on her side. The discipline lasted about two seconds before the baby decided his chin looked like a better target.

He caught Maeve's hand once again, only this time held it as he said, "There was more to it than Daphne's decision to go vegan. The old man thought she was betraying all the ranchers around here when she put in this animal sanctuary."

Callie shot him a look of puzzlement. "But why? She's not hurting you ranchers. She's saving animals' lives."

"True. But the way the old man sees it, ranchers sell their cattle for meat. To put food on family tables. Daphne's farm represents saving all animals."

Callie frowned. "But you're a rancher. You've come to visit the farm and you're even going to give her a donation. Obviously you don't see her and this farm as a threat."

Smiling wanly, he shook his head. "The

few cows that come to live here on Happy Hearts are not going to hurt the Flying A, or any other ranch around here, for that matter. And someone needs to take care of these castoffs. My family appreciates Daphne's effort."

"Hmm. Daphne's father didn't want her to have this farm," Callie mused aloud. "How sad."

"Yeah. With all his money, he could've easily supported her effort. But I doubt he's ever come forward to offer her a penny. Although, I heard that the money Daphne's mother gave her to start up this place was money she'd gotten through her divorce from Cornelius. In any case, I hate to imagine myself ever being that narrow-minded with my daughter."

Callie smiled at him. "Daphne is right, you know. You are a thoughtful man."

He cleared his throat. "Daphne was just being nice. She doesn't really know me."

Callie couldn't imagine what he meant by that remark and the self-deprecating tone in his voice prevented her from asking. Clearly, he didn't like anyone giving him compliments. It was as though he didn't feel worthy of any sort of praise. That made no sense. He was a good man. How could he believe that he wasn't?

The notion saddened Callie, but she did her best to push it out of her mind and put on her cheeriest smile. "What do you say we go find some animals to show Maeve?"

"Sounds good to me."

She reached for his hand and the tender glance he cast her made her forget everything except his strong, warm fingers wrapped around hers.

"Remember? I'm supposed to hold your hand the whole time," she reminded him. "Because of the ghosts."

Chuckling lowly, he squeezed her fingers. "With you holding on to me, I won't be frightened."

They walked over to the barnyard where Maeve immediately caught sight of a potbellied pig roaming freely around the grounds.

"Ahhh-eee!" She squealed and pointed to the animal.

"That's Tiny Tim," Callie told the baby. "He's a sweet pig."

Amused, Tyler shook his head. "You mean eating sweets, don't you? If you ask me, his name should be XL Tim."

"Is that some sort of pig breed—XL?" Callie asked.

He laughed outright. "No, XL for extra-large size."

Callie chuckled. "You're right about the size, but XL just doesn't have the same ring to it."

For the next hour, they wandered around the farm, letting Maeve experience the array of birds and animals. By the time they strolled back to the main barn, the baby had fallen asleep, her head pillowed against Tyler's shoulder.

Most of the other guests had finished their visit to the farm and driven away. Daphne, along with a pair of staff members, had already begun the evening chores.

With a feed bucket in hand, the strawberry-blonde walked over to where Callie and Tyler stood near the door of the barn.

"Are you three leaving?" she asked.

"Yes. It will be dark soon and Maeve is asleep," Callie told her.

Tyler said, "My daughter had so much fun with the animals that she wore herself out."

"I'm glad she enjoyed it." Daphne leveled a pointed look at him. "And thank you, Tyler, for coming. I imagine you have an idea of what it means to me to have a rancher visit this farm. You've made my day, honestly."

"It was my pleasure." He retrieved a wallet from the back pocket of his jeans and pulled out a check. Handing it to her, he said, "Here's a little gift from the Flying A."

She glanced at the check and Callie was amazed to see the woman's blue eyes glaze over with moisture. "Thank you, Tyler. And please thank the rest of your family for me."

"Sure thing."

Daphne cleared her throat and then gave them a big smile. "Before you leave, I have a question. Has either of you seen Maggie around town? We've been hunting everywhere for her."

"Maggie?" Tyler asked blankly.

The name suddenly registered with Callie. "Oh, you're talking about the border collie that won the Bronco Pet Contest during the Fourth of July celebration. Van told me that she went missing."

Daphne's nod was grim. "Technically, the pet contest was on the fifth of July. Maggie won the crown then promptly ran away. I suppose her dash for freedom was her way of saying she didn't want to be the queen of pets."

Tyler glanced at both women. "I hate to sound gruesome, but after this length of time, she might have been struck by a car and killed."

Shaking her head, Daphne gazed wistfully out at the road that ran by the Happy Hearts' property. "You're not being gruesome, you're being realistic. The thought has been crossing my mind ever since she ran away. But so far no one has found her on the highway, or any of the country roads around here. I keep hoping she's still roaming around town and finding scraps to eat. Anyway, if you do see her, please let me know. Everyone here on the farm wants her back. She's a border collie and Australian shepherd mix with long white hair and a brown spot over one eye."

Tyler and Callie assured her they'd keep an eye out for the pooch and then said their goodbyes.

The drive to town passed with minimal conversation. Callie mostly gazed out at the countryside rapidly being cloaked with the shadows of twilight. Tyler kept his focus on the road, trying not to mull on his growing desire for Callie.

When the idea to visit Happy Hearts had first entered Tyler's mind, he'd thought the trip would be a nice, harmless way to give Maeve some enjoyment and him a chance to spend a little time with Callie. Now he had to admit to himself that the simple outing had turned out to be all those things and more.

Something about being on the farm and watching Callie and Maeve enjoying the animals together, almost like a real mother and daughter, had touched Tyler in a way he'd not expected. Even his cynical eyes could see that Callie was growing close to his daughter and that Maeve was forming a bond with her. He had to be pleased about the development. His daughter needed a woman's touch. Even more than what his mother gave her during babysitting stints. Yet he couldn't deny he felt a bit uneasy about the change in their lives.

He had no idea how long this thing with Callie might last. In fact, he was beginning to wonder how soon she was going to tire of his effort to keep the growth of their relationship at a snail's pace. There were times, when she thought he wasn't looking, that he'd spotted a flash of frustration in her eyes. And he didn't need for her to tell him in so many words that she was waiting for him to move things forward, to take their relationship to a deeper level. He could sense her disappointment each time he ended their kisses before they had a chance to get heated.

Hell, any normal man would've already taken her into his bed, Tyler thought. But he wasn't normal. No, there was something inside him that was scarred and twisted, and too afraid to ever believe he could be truly happy again.

Chapter Seven

Maeve had fallen asleep by the time they'd reached Callie's apartment. Tyler carried her inside and Callie followed with the child's diaper bag.

"Poor baby," Callie said softly as they walked the short hallway to the living room. "She's gone to sleep without any dinner."

"We'll feed her when she wakes," he assured her.

After removing his black Stetson and placing it on the coffee table, he went over to the armchair where the baby usually slept, and was about to place her on the cushion when Callie suddenly stopped him.

"Wait, Tyler. Before you put Maeve down in the chair, I have something to show you."

She motioned for him to follow her along the hallway toward the bedroom.

Tyler's brows shot up at the idea of being inside her room. "Show me what?" he asked skeptically.

She pulled a playful face at him. "Don't ask questions. Just come this way."

When she entered her bedroom, he paused at the door, reluctant to go any farther. She might as well have been asking Tyler to enter a lions' den without so much as a whip for protection.

Seeing he was standing in the open doorway with no intentions of moving, she said in an exasperated voice, "Come in. I have something for Maeve."

He followed her over to a corner of the shadowy room. And then he saw it. A white, portable, baby crib, complete with a mobile of small animals and colorful tinkling bells.

Tyler stared at the baby bed in stunned fascination. "Where did you get this?" he asked.

She placed the diaper bag on a dressing bench. "I found it in a furniture store in Bronco Valley," she said.

He was overwhelmed that she'd gone to all this trouble and expense for Maeve, and for him. "You shouldn't have done this, Callie. In fact, I'm going to insist on paying you for it."

A horrified expression came over her face and Tyler realized he would have to be careful about what he said next. Otherwise, he might crush her feelings. And hurting Callie was the last thing he wanted.

She hurried over to his side. "You're not going to do any such thing! It's my gift to Maeve. She deserves to have a nice bed while she's here at the apartment. Go ahead and put her in it. The sheets and blanket are just washed."

Feeling certain he was losing a battle that he probably shouldn't have started in the first place, Tyler gently laid Maeve in the crib.

Once she was resting on her back in the middle of the crib, he slipped off her shoes.

"Could you hand me a diaper from her bag?" he asked. "I should've changed her before we left the farm. But she'll never know it now."

Callie dug out a diaper from the stuffed bag and carried it back to him.

"Let me do it," she said. "When Van and Jameson have a baby, she might ask me to babysit for her. I can't do that without any diaper-changing experience."

At least she hadn't said whenever she had a baby of her own, Tyler thought.

"Go for it," he said, stepping to one side to make room for her. "You've watched me do it enough to know how."

"It looks simple enough. And now that I'm not afraid to handle her, I'm pretty sure I can manage."

Slowly and gently, she removed Maeve's damp diaper and handed it to him. "I'll let you put this in the trash can. There's one in the bathroom—in the corner right behind you."

"Mighty generous of you," he said with humorous sarcasm.

He fastened the dirty diaper into a tight roll and carried the bundle to the bathroom. When he returned to the crib, Callie had already gotten the fresh diaper fastened on Maeve and was in the process of covering her with a light blanket.

"Still asleep," she said proudly. "And see how comfy she looks on her new bed."

He turned away from the crib and gently placed his hands on her shoulders. How could he explain that her gift to Maeve felt like a tender trap to him? He couldn't.

"Callie, I, uh, I don't know what to say. You—"

Callie wrapped a hand around his upper arm and tugged him a few steps back from the crib.

"Listen, Tyler, I don't want you to take this all wrong. I didn't buy a bed for Maeve just to make brownie points with you. This doesn't mean I'm trying to throw a lasso around you or anything like that. It just means that I love Maeve and I wanted to do this for her. Okay?"

Dear God, she must be able to read his mind, he thought. And as he studied her for long moments, old memories of Maeve's constant crying and Luanne's shrill demands pushed their way into his thoughts and sent a shiver down his spine. What if Callie suddenly changed into a woman he didn't recognize? What if Maeve reverted to being a cranky, miserable child? The whole nightmare would start all over again.

Don't be stupid, Tyler. Callie could never be like Luanne. And Maeve has grown out of those colicky days and nights. The future could be good. If you'd only give it a chance.

Shoving the voice in his head aside, he drew in a deep breath. "Okay," he said finally. "But what if—"

When he didn't go on, he could see a shadow of disappointment fall over her face. Damn it, why couldn't he just thank her and keep his mouth shut? Why did he have to make things complicated? Because most of his married life had been complicated?

She swallowed then said, "If we decide not to date each other anymore? Isn't that what you're trying to ask?"

He answered with a rueful nod, but instead of appearing frustrated with him, she gave him a bright smile. "Then I'll put the crib away and save it for when I have a child of my own. See? One way or the other, the little bed won't go to waste."

The mere mention of her saving this crib for when she gave birth to some other man's child grated over Tyler like a piece of coarse-grit sandpaper. But she couldn't know that. How could she? He could hardly admit to himself, much less to her, that he was thinking of her in a possessive way. Besides, she was being so casual about it all that Tyler felt like an idiot for putting up a protest in the first place.

"I am grateful to you, Callie. And I honestly don't deserve you—or the way you make me feel."

Her eyelids lowered just enough to send a prickle of awareness rushing through him.

"How do I make you feel?" she asked softly.

Without thinking, he pulled her close, pressed her against him. "Like a man. A very hungry man."

Her lips parted and her soft sigh brushed against the side of his face. The caressing sensation was more than he could stand and before he could tamp down the feelings raging inside him, he wrapped his arms around her and covered her lips with his.

She clearly understood that this embrace was nothing like the tepid kisses he'd been giving her these past few days when he'd been holding back, worrying, tossing around the pros and cons of having an affair. But not now. He was kissing her like a starved man and they were both feeling the flames wrapping them tightly together.

The hungry search he made of her lips

went on for so long that Tyler's lungs felt as though they were being crushed and white lights appeared behind his closed eyes.

Forced to refuel his body with oxygen, he broke the contact of their lips. As he sucked in deep breaths and tried to control the hammering of his heart, Callie's head lolled limply backward. Her dark hair slipped away from the creamy column of her neck and Tyler was quick to take advantage of the exposed skin.

As he planted tiny, butterfly kisses beneath her ear and down the side of her neck, she groaned with pleasure.

"Tyler. Please keep kissing me. Touching me."

Her husky plea was like a kiss unto itself and the need to make love to her ratcheted up another notch as his lips took a downward slide to the curve of her shoulder and finally onto the ridge of her collarbone. She tasted sweet and delicious, and he wondered how long this would have to go on before he got his fill. Hours? Days? No, he couldn't imagine that being nearly enough time to enjoy the pleasures of her body.

"You don't have to ask, sweet Callie. Just hang on to me. Let me taste you. Feel you. Everywhere."

As he whispered the words against her warm skin, he could feel a shiver pass through her body. It mirrored the rush of sensations that had started in his head and traveled rapidly downward to his loins. Now they were burning, begging his hands to drag her hips against the erection that was already pressing against his jeans.

He felt her arms slip around him, her body align itself to his and, at that moment, as her breasts yielded to his chest, Tyler recognized that he was totally lost to her. He was beyond the point of being able to pull back, to walk away. No matter the consequences.

"Callie…" he murmured against her cheek. "I've wanted this—you—for…oh, I don't know…it feels like forever."

"And I've wanted you," she said thickly.

"But I thought you didn't want to make love to me."

Just hearing her say the words elicited a guttural groan deep in his throat. "I must've been doing some great acting because making love to you is all I've been wanting."

"Then show me what you're feeling. That's what I really want."

He lowered his mouth to hers and, using his lips and tongue, kissed her until she began to whimper with need and he was close to exploding.

Pulling slightly back from her, he rubbed his thumbs over the rigid nipples pushing against the fabric of her tank top. "I think we should get undressed, don't you?"

She nodded and a slice of sanity had him glancing toward the open doorway. "What about Van?" he asked huskily. "Will she be coming home tonight?"

Her eyes were drowsy as she smiled up at him. "No. Lucky for us, she's staying at Jameson's tonight. Or lucky for him," she added wickedly. "Whichever way you want to look at it."

Chuckling, he said, "I'd say we're lucky all the way around."

The news that they would have the apartment all to themselves had him tugging the hem of her tank top from the waistband of her jeans. She promptly lifted her arms and he pulled the garment over her head and tossed it on the dressing bench next to Maeve's diaper bag.

Without a moment's pause to glance at her scantily covered breasts, he removed her jeans and ankle boots, then stepped back to take in the sexy image of her standing in a set of lacy black lingerie.

A lopsided grin twisted his lips. "I wasn't expecting to find this," he admitted.

A breathless laugh rushed out of her. "What were you expecting? Pantaloons and a corset?"

His hands cupped the firm breasts swathed in lace then slipped down her rib cage and onto the flare of her hips. "Nothing quite this naughty. I'm beginning to think you have another side to you."

"I have all kinds of sides to me," she whispered. "If you care to look for them."

Groaning, he brushed his lips against hers. "I'm looking, Callie girl."

By the time he planted another long, heated kiss to her mouth, she was reaching to undo the pearl snaps on his shirt. He let her open them before he circled his hands around both her wrists.

"The bedroom door," he said. "I'm going to shut and lock it. Just in case Van decides to come home for some reason."

"Okay. I want you to feel comfortable," she told him.

After dealing with the door, he returned to where she was standing by the side of the bed. Her brown eyes filled with a soft, inviting light as she gazed up at him.

"Is there a chance we might wake Maeve?" she asked.

"The only thing that will wake Maeve is

hunger, a wet diaper, or maybe an earth-quake."

The corners of her lips tilted temptingly up-ward as she reached to undo his belt buckle. "The diaper is taken care of for a while. But we don't know when she might get hungry or if an earthquake might rattle us. That means we'd better speed things up."

Tyler had planned to give her all the time she needed to undress him. But the more her hands brushed against his chest and down to the flesh beneath his navel, it was more than he could stand.

"Let me finish this, Callie," he whispered. "It'll be faster."

He tugged off his boots then hurriedly did away with his clothing. When he was finally down to nothing but a pair of black boxers, she reached for his hand and pulled him down alongside her on the bed.

Feeling like he'd fallen into a steamy dream, Tyler drew her into his arms until her warm body was clamped tight against his and his mouth was making a feast of hers.

Desire was shooting through him like a red-hot comet, leaving a wake of sizzling heat all the way from the top of his head to the soles of his feet. He couldn't ever remember a time when he'd felt this much, wanted this much. He was consumed with need, and Callie was the only one to fill him up and make the ache go away.

Tearing his mouth from hers, he turned his attention to removing her bra and panties. The sight of her completely naked, with her rosy-brown nipples puckered into hard buds and her thighs slightly parted, was enough to send him over the edge. But somehow he contained himself enough to cup a hand around one small breast.

Then a thought struck him and he sat straight up on the edge of the bed and muttered a curse under his breath.

"This is bad," he said. "Really bad."

Dazed, she sat up in the middle of the bed. "What? What's wrong?"

He turned a helpless look on her. "I wasn't, uh, planning on this, Callie. I don't have any condoms with me. Hell, I haven't needed those things in...well, years."

She appeared crestfallen, but he could've told her that her disappointment couldn't begin to match his.

"Oh," she said. "I'd forgotten about us needing protection. There's a drugstore—" The rest of her sentence was forgotten as a smile of triumph suddenly lit her face. "No worries, Tyler. Just give me a minute."

She scooted off the bed and pattered into the bathroom. Tyler stared wondrously after her, thinking she must have her own method of birth control tucked away.

He was wrong.

Less than a minute later, she emerged from the bathroom carrying a small box of condoms.

"Is that what I think it is?"

Her cheeks turned pink as she smothered a laugh behind her hand. "It is. Now one of us won't have to run to the corner drugstore."

She handed him the box and he noticed

the safety seal was still intact. "This hasn't been opened."

Her cheeks turned even pinker. "No. I never had any reason to open it. You see, they were going to be a gift. I thought Zach and I would be spending a cozy little Christmas together. But we never even got as close as a kiss beneath the mistletoe. He lit out long before the holiday celebrations started."

What could he say? Except that he was glad for the condoms and glad the jerk who'd left her was out of her life for good.

He opened the box and darted a wry glance at her. "You must have been planning on lots of celebrating."

"Not exactly," she said. "They were cheaper by the dozen."

Laughing, he tossed the box to one side and pulled her into his arms. "Oh, Callie, you're something special."

She curled her arms tightly around his neck and kissed him until the need in both of them had him reaching for one of the condoms.

Once he was wearing the protection, he

eased her down on the bed and parted her thighs. Gently, his fingers brushed the outer flesh before he slowly slipped them into the warm, intimate folds of her womanhood.

Beyond the roaring in his ears, he heard her tiny moan before she arched against his hand, taking his fingers in deeper.

"Oh, Tyler, love me. Love me."

Her voice was strangled, but at least she could speak. Tyler couldn't have uttered a word if he'd tried. It was all he could do to hang on to his self-control. Otherwise, everything was going to end before it ever started.

He stroked her until she was whimpering and writhing against him, and then suddenly the urge to taste her overpowered every thought, every burning need inside him.

Dropping his head, he touched his lips to that intimate part of her and when she cried out with need, he understood that she was feeling just as desperate and vulnerable as he was. The thought bound him to her in a way he'd never experienced before and he wondered if something had clicked in his brain. Or was it his heart that was going through a major upheaval? He didn't know. He couldn't know. All he knew was that she tasted like paradise.

But the need to connect his body to hers soon had him lifting his head. When he positioned himself to enter her, she opened her eyes and smiled at him.

"Callie." Her name was all he could squeeze past the hot lump in his throat, but at this point, he didn't think either of them needed words between them. This was all about a man and woman communicating in the most fundamental way. About giving and taking until there was no longer two of them, but only one.

"I want you," she whispered.

Those were the only words she spoke as he entered her with one steady thrust. After that, Tyler doubted he could have heard anything. As her warm body enveloped him, he felt certain someone had shot him off into space. Surely, he thought, no one could feel like this and still be on earth.

But then she began to move beneath him and Tyler's body instinctively responded. In a matter of moments, he was mindlessly driving into her.

Somewhere in the grip of desire, he felt her hands roaming over his back, along his rib cage and down to his hips. The scent of her skin filled his head, while her short, raspy breaths were like an aphrodisiac on his senses.

He needed more time, he thought. To slide his lips over every inch of her skin, to pull the budded nipples of her breasts into his mouth, to feel her thighs and the very essence of her womanhood tightening around him. But with each passing second, his control crumbled more and more.

When it finally snapped, he was caught up on a giant wave of ecstasy that swept him higher and higher. Somewhere from afar he heard Callie cry his name and felt her hips arch desperately toward his. They were reaching the euphoric spot of their journey at the same time and the realization spun his senses into a whirlwind. The helpless feeling that he was going to float completely away had him gripping Callie tightly to him. And Tyler didn't let go until the room stopped spinning and he could breathe again.

Long moments passed before Callie managed to open her eyes and, even then, she was too dazed to understand what had just occurred. Was that the way sex was supposed to be?

She'd thought she had known how it felt to have a man pleasure her body. But she couldn't have been more ignorant. Until this moment, she would've never comprehended the fact that making love to Tyler could transport her to another dimension. She hadn't known that time would stand still and she would become utterly lost to Tyler's lips and hands, adrift in a hazy cloud of bliss.

No. She hadn't expected to feel as though she'd been flying among the stars, but she had. And what was he thinking? Had he felt the same reckless pleasure she'd experienced?

Shifting beneath the partial weight of his body, she rolled to her side so that she was facing him. His eyes were closed, his features slack. He looked like a man who'd been running for a long time and had finally found a safe haven to rest. And as her gaze drowsily took in the black lashes resting against his cheeks, the curve of his lips, a pang of tender longing filled her chest and stung her eyes with hot moisture.

When his eyelids eventually lifted, his gaze met hers and, without a word, he tugged her tight in his arms and buried his face in the curve of her neck.

Blinking fiercely, she clung to him and tried not to think beyond this night.

"Callie, I—I'm sorry."

Her heart, which had been chugging at a fast pace, very nearly sputtered to a stop. "Sorry?" she murmured. "For what?"

He lifted his head and as his eyes met hers,

he smoothed the tumbled strands of hair off her forehead.

"For not making everything better for you. I wanted to make this special. But I guess I've forgotten how to make love to a woman."

The relief that flooded through her was followed by a real need to reassure him and she used the tips of her fingers to trace a tender track along his jaw. "Tyler, you have nothing to be sorry for. Everything was incredible. And so very special. It couldn't have been any better for me."

A long sigh eased out of him and then he rubbed his cheek against hers. "Like I said before. I don't deserve you."

Now wasn't the moment to press him for an explanation of his feelings. She didn't want anything to ruin this intimate time with him. Later on, if he grew to care for her enough, he might allow the secrets in his heart to come pouring out. Until then, having him in her arms and in her bed had to be enough.

Tightening her arm against his back, she whispered, "I think you need to turn that around, Tyler. It might be that I don't deserve you."

Easing his head back, he stared at her in disbelief. "That's a crazy statement."

"No crazier than yours," she replied. "You're an Abernathy. You're from an old, established, wealthy family of Bronco Heights. I'm Callie Sheldrick from Bronco Valley. My mother deals with insurance customers all day long and most of the time my dad has a nail gun in his hands. We're simple people."

"My family is simple, too, Callie. Owning land and livestock doesn't really make us any different. We still have to work to make a living. Just like you and your family."

Sighing, she smiled and pushed her fingers through the dark brown hair above his ear. He'd never understand, and maybe it was best that way, she thought.

"If you say so," she said quietly.

"I do. And there's one other little thing I need to say."

"Tell me."

A quirk of a smile lifted one corner of

his lips. "I'm glad you decided they were cheaper by the dozen."

Laughing softly, she pulled her head down to his and let her lips do the rest of her talking.

Tyler stood outside the big horse barn at the Flying A and carefully watched as Dean lead the palomino around in a wide circle.

"Sandman is limping, all right," Tyler told his brother. "Front left. Are you sure he doesn't have a stone lodged in his frog or shoe?"

Dean slowly led the horse over to where Tyler was standing in the shade of the building. Although the morning sun was barely peeping over the distant mountains, the temperature was already climbing. They were going to have a hot day moving cattle from the bottomland, where a stretch of drought had already dwindled grazing to nothing.

"I've looked," Dean told him. "You have a go at it. I'm beginning to think the problem is in his ankle."

Tyler squatted and ran both hands over the gelding's ankle. "Doesn't look puffy or feel warm." He stood and picked up the horse's hoof to examine the shoe and the sole of his foot. "You rode Sandman yesterday. When did he start limping?"

"After I saddled him a few minutes ago and led him out of the barn." Dean gave the horse's neck an affectionate pat. "Maybe he's faking it to get out of work today."

"He's not faking." Tyler pulled a hoof pick from the back pocket of his jeans and raked at a clump of hard dirt wedged in the crease next to the frog. "There must be a rock in this."

The dirt clump fell to the ground and broke apart to reveal a piece of sharp rock. Seeing it, Dean groaned. "Damn. How did I miss that?"

"It's easy to do," Tyler replied.

"Thanks, brother. Now I won't have to ride Lumpy."

"Call him Jumpy if you put on your spurs," Tyler reminded him then chuckled. "Or have you forgotten landing in that prickly pear patch?"

Dean directed a sarcastic smirk at him. "Not likely. If I looked hard enough, I'd probably still find a few thorns in my backside."

Tyler headed back into the barn and Dean wrapped Sandman's reins around a hitching post before following his younger brother into the cooler alleyway of the building.

"Think we should go to the house and get Mom to pack us some sandwiches? We might be out until this afternoon," he suggested.

"I have sandwiches in my saddlebags," Tyler told him as he fastened a pair of batwing chaps to his legs. "When I dropped Maeve off, Mom already had them fixed. Bologna and cheese. Your favorite."

"Ha! More like your favorite." Dean feigned a weary sigh. "That's the way it is when you're the baby of the family. Your parents spoil you rotten."

"Sure, Dean." With the chaps snapped in place, he straightened to his full height and looked at his brother. "We're burning daylight. Are you ready?"

"No. I want to talk to you first."

"Talk? We can talk on the ride out to the cattle."

Dean shook his head. "I want your undivided attention. Once we head out, you'll be inspecting the grass, looking at the clouds and the birds, and thinking about everything but what I'm saying."

Tyler folded his arms across his chest and faced his brother. "Okay. What is it? Are you worried about Dad wanting to add more cattle to the Flying A?"

"Well, with a drought setting in, it seems damned risky. But no. Dad has kept this ranch in the black for many years. He knows what he's doing even when it looks like he's making a huge mistake. This is about you," Dean told him.

"Me? What have I done?" Tyler wanted to know.

"Nothing."

"Then why are we having this conversation? Dean, sometimes I wonder about you. You're as quiet as a church mouse with everyone else—except me. Now what gives with that?"

Dean grimaced. "You're the baby of the bunch. You need the guidance of an older brother. And I am six years older than you. So that makes me wiser."

"Wiser. Really?" Tyler asked sarcastically.

"All right. Maybe I'm not smarter than you. But I'm not about to get myself into girl trouble."

Tyler's brows quirked. "Girl trouble? What are you talking about?"

"I've had several acquaintances of ours tell me they've been seeing you all over town with the little brunette."

Tyler bristled. "She has a name, Dean. It's Callie. Callie Sheldrick. And, yeah, we've been going out—and we always have Maeve with us. Just in case you're thinking I've been leaving my daughter with Mom every night."

The heated tone of Tyler's voice took Dean

by surprise. "What the hell is wrong with you? I'm not thinking anything of the sort."

"Then what's worrying you? Only a couple of weeks ago you told me how glad you were that I was going out again. That I had found a woman who interested me. Now you're thinking I'm headed for trouble."

"Yeah, I told you I was happy about you getting back into the land of the living. But I didn't have any idea you were going to leap into the frying pan. From what I hear, the two of you are practically engaged and Maeve is calling this woman mommy."

Cursing under his breath, Tyler stalked a few steps away from his brother then paced right back. "That's stupid! Maeve is nine months old. She can't say words yet, much less 'mommy.' And as for Callie and I being close to getting engaged—that's crazy. I've not known her long enough to make that kind of commitment!"

Dean stared at him in wonder. "You hardly worried about that with Luanne. You married her after a few short weeks."

Tyler's back teeth snapped together. "Damn it, Dean. Don't bring her into this. None of it is your business anyway. So butt out!"

Sighing, Dean rubbed a hand across his forehead. "Sorry. I guess it isn't any of my business. I just don't want to see my brother jumping into something that might hurt him down the road. You've gone through enough pain, Tyler. And I think you should consider Callie in all of this, too. If you're not really interested in something long-term with her, then it isn't fair to make her feel as though she's part of your little family."

But she was part of it, Tyler thought. She and Maeve were his family. Maybe not in the legal sense, but in every other way. Callie treated Maeve as though she was her own daughter. And she treated Tyler like— His mind suddenly halted at the word *husband*.

When the two of them had first made love a little more than a week ago, Tyler had been stunned by the depth of his reaction to her. He hadn't expected the onslaught of emotions that had poured through him. He hadn't thought he could ever feel that much. And he'd especially been shocked that he'd given so much of himself to her.

Taking their relationship to a deeper level had not been something he'd planned. It had simply happened. And right or wrong, he'd been going around in a happy daze because of Callie. Because she made him feel like he'd never felt in his entire life. And it wasn't just the incredible sex they shared. She was kind and sweet and thoughtful. She understood things about him that no one else seemed to notice or care about.

"Look, Dean, Callie understands that I'm not ready for any kind of commitment."

"Does she?" He shrugged and shook his head. "If you two are just sharing a few laughs over some meals, then she probably does understand. But if you're letting her believe your intentions are serious, then you're treading on thin ice."

Annoyed as hell that Dean was getting too close to the truth, he snapped. "What would you know about it, anyway?" Tyler demanded. "You've never been married or had a child! You've never been a widower, either. How could you possibly know what I'm feeling or what I need?"

"You're right," his brother muttered. "I can't know." Dean turned on his heel and walked out of the barn.

Tyler heaved a breath of frustration and wearily pinched the bridge of his nose. His brother was only trying to help him. But Dean didn't understand that, for the first time in years, Tyler felt wanted. And the feeling was too good to give up. For now, at least.

Giving himself a hard, mental shake, he walked out of the barn and over to where Dean was tightening the cinch on Sandman's saddle.

Laying an affectionate hand on his brother's shoulder, he said in a mollified voice, "Sorry, Dean, for going off like I did. I shouldn't have been so touchy."

Dean buckled the cinch and tucked the excess end in its holder. "Don't worry about it. We're brothers. We should be able to say what we think without having to apologize for it later."

"Yeah, well, I get it. You're trying to give me advice because you love me."

Glancing over his shoulder, Dean gave him a wry grin. "You think I love you, huh? Where'd you ever get that idea?"

Tyler chuckled. "Oh, probably when Bobby Landry broke my nose in a fight on the school grounds and you tracked him down and broke his."

Dean laughed out loud. "You were in fifth grade and Bobby Landry was my age. He was a big bully with you smaller boys. You actually remember that I broke his nose?"

"I remember everything."

"Good. Then you won't forget that half of those bologna sandwiches Mom made are mine."

A few minutes later, as the two brothers rode side by side across the open prairie, Tyler wasn't taking in the majestic outline of mountains in the distance, the fluffy bits of cloud drifting across the blue horizon, or the sound of sagebrush popping against the horses' legs. Dean had planted too many questions in Tyler's mind. Questions he wasn't ready to answer.

Was he purposely letting Callie believe his plans for her were serious? Was making love to her the same as misleading her? For the past week and a half, he'd spent every night at her apartment and in her bed. But the notion that she might be getting the wrong idea about his intentions had never crossed Tyler's mind. Why should it? He'd never mentioned the word *love* to her. He'd never discussed his future goals, or that he might want her to be part of them.

Oh, Tyler, love me. Love me.

Those words had been said to him in a rush of heated passion. She'd meant them only in a physical sense. At least, that was how he'd interpreted her whispered plea. But now he was beginning to wonder if she was truly developing a deep attachment to him.

And what if she is, Tyler? Don't you want Callie's love? Don't you want to envision the future with her at your side? The two of you building a family together?

No! he mentally shouted back at the voice in his head. He couldn't accept Callie's love. He'd been a worthless husband the first time and if he tried to make a second go of it, there were no guarantees he'd be any better.

Besides, Tyler had no right to a happy future. He'd lost that privilege when he'd allowed Luanne to run out in the night and never come back.

Chapter Eight

Usually, Callie stopped by her parents' home once a week at least, to say hello and catch up on family news. And, occasionally, when she had time to spare, she'd pop into the insurance office where her mother worked and take her to lunch. But Callie had been so tied up with her job and seeing Tyler in her spare time that two weeks had slipped by without her realizing she'd done neither.

A few minutes ago, when Patricia Sheldrick had showed up at Bronco Ghost Tours and announced she was there to take her daughter to lunch, Callie had been pleasantly surprised.

Now, as the two women sat at a sunny table in Bronco Java and Juice, Callie plied her mother with questions.

"Has Dad been busy? I heard an investor wants to build another apartment complex in Bronco Valley. But you can hear anything and everything in this town."

"Martin has had plenty of work. In fact, he's not had a day off in two weeks. You know how it is with builders. Wait, wait, wait for supplies to arrive then hurry like crazy to meet the contract deadline."

As a child, Callie had grown accustomed to having her father home for several days running, or not seeing him at all. The construction business was never predictable. "Well, what about Dakota? Have you talked to her lately? I suppose she's still living with Buster."

Frowning with disapproval, Patricia reached for her coffee.

As Callie watched her carefully sip the hot

drink, she thought how her looks were the exact opposite of her mother's wheat-blonde hair and sky-blue eyes. Instead, Callie was a feminine version of her father. She'd been born with his same dark hair and brown eyes.

"Callie," Patricia scolded, "you know very well the guy's name is Roderick."

"And Dakota calls him Roddy. What a wimp," Callie said with obvious sarcasm. "When is she going to realize he's a loser? They've been living together for—how long?—nearly two years, and he still hasn't asked her to marry him. Strange how he'll let her support him on her nursing wages, though."

"Callie! What in the world is going on with you? It isn't like you to carry on about your sister's private life. Dakota is going on thirty years old. She's big enough to decide what is or isn't good for her."

"Well, you can't be happy with her situation," Callie argued.

Patricia took another sip of coffee before she replied. "Your dad and I don't necessarily approve of Roddy, but we think she needs to figure things out for herself. We're hoping she'll open her eyes to him."

Callie thoughtfully chewed a bite of her sandwich and followed it with a swig of lemonade. "As sisters, we've never really been alike. I can't expect Dakota to think like me. Besides, sometimes I think—"

Patricia leveled a questioning look at her daughter. "You think what, honey?"

Callie grimaced. "That I need to open my own eyes."

"Regarding?"

Across the busy room, Callie spotted Cassidy Ware, the owner of Bronco Java and Juice. The petite blonde was not only pretty, she was also a bundle of sass. Cassidy had been the first of Callie's friends to congratulate her when Zach walked out of her life. Apparently, she'd figured out long before Callie had that the guy was a loser. It would be interesting to know Cassidy's opinion on Tyler, she thought.

To her mother she said, "Oh, everything.

My friends say I'm too ready to give people the benefit of the doubt."

"You're talking about men now," Patricia said knowingly. "And I don't think your comment was directed at your ex-boyfriend."

"No. How did you guess?"

Smiling faintly, Patricia shook her head. "Like you said a few moments ago, people in this town talk. I've heard that you've been seeing Tyler Abernathy. You've failed to mention this news to your parents, I might add."

Callie's cheeks grew warm. "Sorry, Mom. But it's all happened so quickly and…" She paused and shrugged as she tried to choose the right words to explain her relationship with Tyler. Not that there was a right way. She was crazy about the guy and he…well, she didn't have a clue how he honestly felt about her.

"Callie, you're having trouble finishing your sentences. That tells me you're uncertain about this man, or yourself."

Uncertain didn't begin to describe what

Callie had been feeling these past days. She'd believed that being intimate with Tyler would make him open up. But as each day passed with him being a closed book, she was beginning to doubt that this thing between them would ever evolve into something deeper and more meaningful. She was probably going to end up just like Dakota, she thought morosely. Giving herself to a man who wouldn't commit.

She sighed heavily. "I'm beginning to be uncertain about both of us."

Patricia studied her daughter's face. "Why? Because he has a baby? And you're not sure you're ready for motherhood right now?"

"Oh no. It's not that at all. I'm getting more and more comfortable with the baby. In fact, I've fallen in love with little Maeve."

Patricia keenly studied her daughter's face. "And what about the baby's father? Have you fallen in love with him?"

Fallen? She'd tumbled wildly head-over-heels for Tyler. But she wasn't ready to admit to her mother that she'd let her emotions get away from her so quickly and recklessly.

"Mom, since you've been hearing gossip, I'm sure you already know that Tyler is a widower. His wife died a little more than six months ago."

"I have heard. In fact, I remember when the accident happened. It was a strange, rather senseless tragedy."

Pricked with curiosity, Callie asked, "How do you mean?"

"Well, it happened rather late at night. No one ever really knew why the woman would be driving the highway at such an hour. And when the highway patrol ruled it an accident from falling asleep at the wheel, the whole incident seemed even more weird. If she was that exhausted, why would she have left the house? Why would her husband have allowed her to leave? But I imagine he's already told you all about the accident."

Callie felt dejected, even though there was really no cause for her to think that way. For all she knew, Tyler probably thought Callie knew all the particulars about his late wife's death and felt no need to rehash the painful facts.

"Actually, Tyler hasn't explained anything about his wife's accident to me. And I haven't wanted to pry. Frankly, he's never uttered her name to me."

Puzzled, Patricia frowned. "I find that rather odd, don't you?"

"I really couldn't say. Some people find it difficult to talk about loved ones they've lost." Or perhaps Tyler still loved his wife so much that he couldn't bear mentioning her name. The idea weighed on Callie's heart.

"Hmm. You could be right." Patricia picked up her sandwich then lowered it to her plate as she leveled a concerned look at Callie. "Well, in any case, Luanne Abernathy hadn't been under the influence of drugs or alcohol, so she must've simply fallen asleep."

But why would Tyler's wife have been so exhausted? Callie wondered. Had Luanne been one of those women who pitched in with the ranching chores? Could it be that the double duty of being a ranch woman and new mother had gotten her down? Callie could ask him. But she'd already sensed that the topic of his wife's death was off limits.

Shaking her head, she said, "That's so sad, Mom. I think that's why Tyler hides behind a wall. He hasn't gotten over losing her yet."

Patricia ate a small portion of her sandwich before she replied to Callie's assumption.

"Honey, I'm going to be honest. I can't believe you want to be involved with a man who's still grieving over his lost wife. Building a relationship with a man is hard enough when things are starting out on good footing. He's bringing baggage of past issues into the mix. And some of those problems are the kind that even a woman my age would have trouble dealing with. Don't you think you'd do better by looking elsewhere and finding a man who's starting out fresh, like you?"

"I probably would, Mom," Callie answered with a wistful sigh. "But there's something about Tyler that hits me right here." She touched a finger to the middle of her chest.

"And go ahead and laugh if you want, but I keep getting the feeling that he needs me."

"Oh dear. A woman can't think straight if she believes a man needs her." She smiled and reached across the table to pat the top of Callie's hand. "But you're not a fool, sweetheart. I have faith that you'll eventually see the whole picture regarding this young man and then you'll know exactly what you want."

Callie knew exactly what she wanted right now. But she didn't believe Tyler's wants were headed in the same direction as hers.

"Thanks, Mom."

Patricia smiled. "You're going to make some lucky man a great wife. Just don't try to rush things, Callie. That's the main thing. And speaking of becoming a wife, has Jameson put an engagement ring on Van's finger yet?"

Glad that her mother had veered the conversation away from Tyler, she said, "Not yet. But I expect it to happen soon. She spends far more time at Jameson's ranch than she does at the apartment. And Melanie and Gabe's wedding is at the end of the month. Then Evan and Daphne's at the end of October. Weddings are popping up like spring daffodils," she said in an attempt to sound cheery.

"And I'm sure my little girl is wondering if she'll ever be planning a wedding of her own," Patricia said knowingly.

Callie shrugged. "Who has time for a wedding? I'm too busy trying to talk people into taking ghost tours. In fact, Evan has come up with a new tour surrounding the old Anderson house down by the river. He ran into some old-timers in the coffee shop the other day and they told him a story about a young bride and her husband who'd lived in the house shortly after it had been built. Seems as though he was drafted into the army and was later killed in the Normandy invasion. She was so distraught over losing him, she jumped off her bedroom balcony. Now, every so often, people claim to see her walking around the balcony wearing a long white wedding dress and veil."

"How morbid. I hope Evan made up that story. It's too sad to think such a tragedy really happened."

"Well, ever since the old men related the story to him, Evan has been digging through the archives at the newspaper office, trying to find out if there's a grain of truth to it. The incident would've taken place seventy-five or seventy-six years ago. That's a long time, but you'd think the newspaper would've saved those wartime editions."

Patricia arched a brow. "You sound like you believe he'll actually find an article about the woman."

"I'll say this much, Evan won't build a tour around the place unless there was actually a young bride and a soldier in the war."

Patricia shook her head in wry disbelief. "Callie, it still amazes me that you've ended up working in a business that promotes ghosts and goblins. When you were a little girl, you wouldn't go to sleep unless you had a night-light on in your bedroom. What happened to you?"

Callie laughed. "While I was growing up I must've watched too many campy monster movies. They taught me that none of this supernatural stuff can be real. Evan doesn't necessarily believe it, either. But he appreciates the moneymaking side of it. Guess he gets that from his great-grandmother."

Patricia chuckled. "Now, Callie, don't you believe in Winona Cobbs's predictions?"

The signal is strong. Don't be afraid.

Callie couldn't begin to count the times Winona's strange words of advice had darted through her mind. She even had passing moments when she wondered if the phrases could actually mean something. But then common sense would step in and push the ridiculous notions aside. Winona wasn't really psychic. No one was.

Glancing at her mother, she answered, "About as much as I believe it will snow in Bronco on the Fourth of July."

Bronco Ghost Tours was busy when Callie returned from lunch with her mother, and throughout the remainder of the afternoon, customers continued to come and go in a steady stream.

Callie welcomed the extra work because it made the afternoon whiz by. Not that she didn't like her job. She'd actually grown to love it. But Tyler had promised she'd see him as soon as he wound up his evening chores on the ranch and drove into town. And foolish or not, she couldn't wait to be with him again.

She was more than surprised when she parked her Jeep in front of the apartment complex and spotted Tyler's truck in a nearby parking slot.

The last time they'd been together, Callie had given him a key to her apartment, but she'd not expected him to use it tonight. She'd thought he was going to arrive around seven. How had he managed to get here an hour early?

On the way to her door, she dug the key from her shoulder bag, but the effort proved to be unnecessary. Before she had a chance to insert the key into the lock, the door swung open.

"Hi there, Ms. Sheldrick," he greeted teasingly. "Care to come into *my* apartment?"

His early arrival had already put a smile on Callie's face and finding him in a happy mood lifted her spirits even higher.

"Hi there, yourself," she told him. "And yes, I would like to come into *your* apartment. If you're not too busy to entertain company."

Laughing, he pulled her across the threshold and into his arms. As his lips came down on hers, he pushed the door closed with the toe of his boot. Callie wrapped her arms around his waist and let her lips convey just how glad she was to be back in his embrace.

When he finally lifted his head, she said, "Mmm. Now that's the kind of greeting a girl wants after a hard day at work."

"I'll be sure to remember that." He took her by the arm and led her down the hallway to the kitchen. "Did you have a hard day?"

"We were very busy. Lots of tourists are

driving through Bronco and they appear to be intrigued with the idea of taking a ghost tour." She sniffed at the mouthwatering smell permeating the kitchen. "Did you bring food? What is that?"

"I did bring food," he told her, then added, "I hope you don't mind if we eat here this evening. I'll help clean up the mess."

"Oh, I love the idea of eating here," she told him. "But you should've let me pick up something on my way home. You've been paying for all our meals. It's my turn."

"Don't even think about it, pretty lady. This is a one-way deal. I supply the food."

"If you say so." She moved further into the kitchen and peered around at the dining table. She'd expected to find Maeve strapped in her carrier, but the baby wasn't to be seen. "Where's Maeve? Please don't tell me you left her with your mother."

He shook his head. "Mom and Maeve had a long visit this morning while my brothers and I vaccinated calves. Maeve is in your bedroom, asleep in her crib."

"Aw, and I didn't get to feed her."

"Don't worry. I expect she'll wake up soon." He left her side and walked to the electric range. Pulling a pair of aluminum pans from the oven, he said, "I put the oven on warm so our food wouldn't get cold. I hope you don't mind me making myself at home."

This evening he was dressed in blue jeans so faded they were nearly white and a blue-plaid shirt with a three-cornered tear near the hem. No matter what he wore, he always looked incredibly sexy. But seeing him like this in worn work clothes somehow drew Callie even closer to him. Maybe the fact that he was an Abernathy didn't really put him on an unreachable pedestal, she decided.

"Are you kidding? I want you to feel at home here."

He placed the pans on top of the stove, then walked over to slip his arms around her waist. "I do feel comfortable here in your apartment, Callie. But I've been wondering if— Have you thought about visiting my place on the ranch?"

Callie was so stunned by his suggestion that, for a moment, all she could do was stare at him. "Your home?"

He nodded. "I believe I told you that I have a separate house from my parents. In fact, it's about a mile and half away from the big ranch house."

Joy was making her heart do a crazy jig against her ribs. "Yes, you mentioned it. But I, uh, didn't think you wanted me to visit your place."

"You thought that?" His dark brows drew together. "Why?"

"Well, you've never invited me. You've never even told me what your home is like."

Was that regret she saw in his twisted smile? Was he actually beginning to realize she needed and wanted to share in his personal life?

His hands gently roamed her back. "You go change and wash, or whatever you need to do. I'll fix the table and we'll talk when you get back. Okay?"

She wanted to grab his face with both

hands and kiss him senseless. But seeing he had his mind on eating, she settled for pressing a quick kiss on his chin.

"I'll be right back," she promised.

After she made a quick visit to the bathroom and changed into shorts and a tank top, she hurried back to the kitchen and found the table set and Tyler filling iced glasses with sweet tea.

The smell of Italian food wafted through the air. She peeked into the pans to see spaghetti and meatballs in one and beef raviolis coated with marinara sauce in the other.

"Yum, yum, all of this smells incredible. And where in the world did you find this kind of Italian food in Bronco?" she asked.

"At the back door of DJ's Deluxe," he said slyly.

She laughed. "The back door? Sure, Tyler. In case you've forgotten, DJ's is a barbecue restaurant. I didn't see any Italian food on the menu."

He shot her a smug grin. "Okay, you're right. There aren't any Italian things on DJ's menu. But back when Mel was managing the place she started purchasing this stuff from the food distributor because Gabe loves Italian food. Even though Mel has moved on from managing the restaurant, they still keep it around for him and his friends. Thankfully, I managed to talk the kitchen into preparing a meal for us."

With a wry shake of her head, Callie said, "There's nothing like having friends in high places, I guess."

Chuckling, he took her by the arm and seated her at one of the place settings. "Eat and enjoy," he said.

He sat in the chair that was angled to her left and as they began to fill their plates, Callie said, "You were going to tell me about your place on the Flying A. I'm dying to hear about it. And don't leave anything out."

"All the details, huh? Okay," he said as he forked a mound of spaghetti onto his plate. "In the first place, it's nothing fancy. Just a rambling ranch house built on a hill that overlooks a little creek. The house has four bedrooms and a big kitchen with an industrial-size stove. Gas. Not like the electric you have here in the apartment."

She laughed. "I wouldn't know how to turn it on, much less how to cook on it."

"I could teach you."

His words warmed her heart and she reached over and placed a hand on his forearm. "That would be fun, Tyler."

He chuckled. "Dean says I have no patience when it comes to teaching."

"Oh what does he know?" she teased. "He's only your brother."

Laughing, he said, "I'm afraid Dean is right. I do lose my patience. But I think you'd be an extra-good student."

"Thanks." She tried a bite of ravioli and discovered it was so delicious she had to have another bite before she spoke again. "Tell me more about the house. Does it have a fireplace?"

"It does. In the den. I don't always have time to cut firewood, though, and because wood is limited, I only burn it when the temperature is really cold—like single-digit numbers."

She nodded that she understood, while imagining herself cuddled in Tyler's arms in front of a crackling fire. "Oh my, that sounds warm and cozy. And you have a den along with four bedrooms. The house must be large."

"It is. Far too large for just Maeve and me. But initially I…well, wasn't planning on it being just the two of us."

He's never uttered her name to me.

I find that rather odd, don't you?

Bits of the conversation she'd had with her mother over lunch suddenly came back to Callie. And, for a moment, it felt as though the ghost of Tyler's ex-wife was sitting in the chair opposite her. The notion left her with a sad, creepy feeling, but she tried her best to brush it aside. He'd gone to a lot of trouble to give her a special dinner. She didn't want to ruin it by thinking too much.

"Do you keep horses and cattle at your place?" she asked.

"I only have two small barns. The only animals I have is a pair of horses and a couple of cattle dogs. Otherwise, the rest of the horses and tack we use are kept at the big ranch yard."

She looked at him and smiled. "The image of looking down on a little creek sounds lovely. Does it usually have water?"

"Most of the time. If we're hit with long dry spells, parts of the creek will dry up. We also have several pasture ranges that have no water sources except for what the windmills pump. Checking those and making sure the tanks are full is something we're always doing."

This was the first time he'd openly talked about his home and work. Everything about it and him intrigued her. "Do you do that chore on horseback?"

His lips took on a wry slant. "A couple of the tanks can be reached on an ATV. But my family doesn't use them."

"Because you like to do things the traditional cowboy way?" she asked.

His smile turned full-blown. "The cowboy way is almost always the best way, Callie. Keeping the cattle quiet and content is a big part of preserving their health. Buzzing around or through a herd with a loud machine sends the cattle running and scattering in all directions. Calves get separated from their mothers and the bawling sets in. Whereas, if we ride up quietly on a horse, they simply look at us and go back to grazing."

"I see. Makes sense to me. But I've heard some ranches use helicopters. That sounds very intrusive."

"I suppose some huge operations need helicopters and ATVs to cover more ground. But I'll tell you this, Callie, I'd never want the Flying A to be *that* huge. Just let me be a horse pilot."

She smiled at him. "Does anyone ever call you old-fashioned?"

He let out a short laugh. "Sometimes. And I don't deny it. I do still do most things the way my dad does them. And I don't follow the latest fads in anything. Now you're sitting there thinking you're having dinner with a fuddy-duddy. Right?"

Laughing softly, she said, "Wrong. Fuddy-duddies don't ride horses, do they?"

He chuckled as he forked a ravioli. "I've seen a few at the local rodeo. We call them tinhorns. They only dress the part."

"Well, I'd be the first to admit that I know very little about ranching and livestock. But I'm learning. And the way you've described the Flying A, it sounds beautiful and serene. I would love to see it and your home—whenever you'd like to show me."

"We'll do that soon," he said. Giving her a sultry little wink, he pushed the spaghetti and meatballs toward her. "Try this. You'll want a whole plateful."

Callie wanted a plateful of him. Every day for the rest of her life. But that was a wish she couldn't imagine coming true. Not with Luanne Abernathy's ghost still haunting Tyler's heart.

* * *

Once they'd finished their meal, Tyler kept his promise and helped Callie clean up the kitchen. By then, Maeve had woken up to let them know with a husky squall that she wanted her bottle.

Callie was quick to offer to take care of the baby. After she'd changed Maeve's diaper and fed her the majority of a bottle, Tyler suggested they go outside to the bench in the courtyard.

During the past hour, clouds had moved in and the hot afternoon had turned into a pleasant evening. They sat for a few minutes on the bench, enjoying the falling twilight, until Maeve began to squirm and wanted down on the ground.

Callie scooped the baby off his lap and then carefully stood her on her feet. "Okay, Maeve, show Daddy how you can walk like a big girl," she said as she held on to both of Maeve's hands to balance her.

Maeve squealed and laughed as she took

wobbly steps along the dirt-packed trail in front of the bench.

"She's getting closer to walking." And Callie was getting deeper and deeper under his skin, Tyler thought, as he watched her gently assist his daughter.

If you're letting her believe your intentions are serious, then you're treading on thin ice.

Damn it, why did Dean's words have to come back to haunt him now, Tyler asked himself. The evening was going too well to ruin it by flashing a danger sign in front of his face.

And, anyway, Callie didn't believe his intentions toward her were serious. Not like in-love-with-her serious. He could tell she'd been totally surprised when he'd mentioned showing her his home on the Flying A. She hadn't been expecting anything like that from him. No more than she was expecting him to say he loved her and wanted to marry her. Why would she think something like that, anyway? They'd only been together a short while, he mentally argued.

Callie might be thinking it, Tyler, because you can't keep your hands off her. Spending night after night with her might be giving her the idea that you want to make being in her bed a permanent setup.

"Hey, Callie, look at you! You've turned into a regular little mother!"

The female voice had Tyler glancing around to see Vanessa approaching them from the direction of the parking lot. Seeing Callie trying to keep Maeve standing on her feet had put a wide grin on the woman's face.

"Hi, Van," Tyler greeted. "Come over and watch the acrobatic show."

Laughing, she walked closer until she was standing a few steps away from the bench. "Since when did you decide that babies weren't scary little monsters?" she asked Callie while giving Tyler a conspiring wink.

Callie glanced up at her roommate. "Working with your brother has taught me not to be afraid of anything," she joked, then added, "If you're hungry, there are plenty of yummy leftovers in the fridge."

"Thanks. But Jameson and I are going out to dinner later on," she said. "I just came by to get a few things from the apartment. So you two don't need to worry that I'm going to stick around and intrude on your evening."

Tyler felt a blush crawling up his neck. He had no idea how much Vanessa knew about his relationship with Callie. But the woman wasn't naive. She'd probably already decided that he and her roommate were sleeping together.

"You wouldn't be intruding," Tyler told her. "This is your apartment, too."

"I can only stay for a little while longer," Vanessa said then glanced at her watch. "I need to run or Jameson will be wondering why I'm late. See you two later." She started off in the direction of the apartment then stopped to look back at them. "I almost forgot to tell you. I think I spotted Maggie. The runaway dog from the pet contest."

Tyler and Callie exchanged hopeful glances.

"Where? Here in town?" Callie quickly asked.

"In the alley behind the ghost tour building," Vanessa answered. "I'm not certain it was the real missing Maggie. I only saw a flash of white and then he or she darted behind a trash dumpster and I lost sight of the animal. I told Evan about it so he could keep an eye out around the building. Maybe you and Saundra can watch for her, too."

"We will," Callie told her. "Did you tell Daphne? She's desperate to find that dog."

"I phoned her immediately. She was so excited; I think she was going to send David into town to drive the streets and look for her."

"Maybe he'll get lucky and spot her," Callie said.

"It's going to take some luck to catch that little Houdini," Vanessa said, waving and hurrying on to the apartment.

"I hope my being here isn't pushing Van out of the apartment," Tyler said. "I don't want her to think she needs to make herself scarce just to give us privacy."

Callie slowly walked Maeve over to where

Tyler was sitting and eased down beside him on the bench.

As she situated Maeve to a comfortable position on her lap, she said, "Believe me, you're not bothering Van. Little by little, she's been moving her things to Jameson's ranch. Like I said, it won't be long before I won't have a roommate at all."

Was Callie wondering why he hadn't already asked her to move in with him at the ranch? Tyler wondered.

Considering that he'd been spending every night here, the move would make things more convenient for him. He wouldn't have to leave Callie's bed long before daylight just to get back to the Flying A by five thirty in the morning. But there were far more serious things to consider besides convenience. For one thing, he didn't want to give her the impression that he was moving them a step closer to getting married, or even engaged. And another, what would it do to him to have Callie in his home for a while and then, once she grew dissatisfied with him or the ranch life, watch her move out? No. Tyler had already gone through too much pain to turn around and ask for more.

He was trying to decide how to reply when Maeve suddenly spotted a squirrel a few feet in front of them and began to squeal and shriek with delight.

For the next fifteen minutes, they remained on the bench to let Maeve watch the squirrel and a pair of pesky blue jays that were squawking at the intrusive humans. But darkness soon forced them back inside the apartment.

It wasn't until Maeve had eaten a jar of baby food and fallen asleep that he finally had a chance to pull Callie down on the couch beside him.

"I'm sorry I don't have a TV," Callie told him. "I can bring my laptop in here and stream a movie or something if you'd like."

He chuckled suggestively as his arm came around her shoulder. "You think I'm getting bored?"

She turned her face toward his and Tyler

thought about how looking into her warm brown eyes was far better than anything he could see on a screen.

"I don't know. What do you do when you come in from work on the ranch?" she asked.

"After taking care of Maeve's needs, I shower and eat something, then I usually lie down with a book. And if I'm really tired, I don't even pick up the book. I just go to sleep. Doesn't sound very entertaining, does it?"

"Depends on what you call entertainment," she said with a sly smile. "If you ask me, just sitting here with you is a pretty nice form of it."

She was so warm and soft, and he'd grown so accustomed to her flowery scent that just a whiff of it filled him with erotic thoughts.

"That's sweet of you to say, Callie. But I'm sure you'd rather be out dancing or going to a movie or something fun. We can do that if you'd like."

Her head tilted slightly to one side as she regarded him. "I can't see you out dancing. Not now. Maybe when you were very young."

His lips twisted. "You mean you can't see me having fun. Isn't that closer to what you were trying to say?"

Her expression turned sober as she cupped her palm against the side of his face. "I imagine you were a very fun guy before…life got in the way."

It was obvious that she was talking about his life before he'd become a widower. And it suddenly struck him that, if he was a brave man, this would be the perfect time for him to open up and tell her all about his quick marriage to Luanne. About all the unhappiness during the years they'd been together. And most of all, how everything had ended because of his failure to be a decent father and husband.

Fun? No. He was only twenty-eight, yet it had been years since Tyler had even thought about having any kind of fun in his life. That's what jumping into a hasty marriage had done to him. Now he was going to be paying for his mistakes for the remainder of his life.

He looked away from her and swallowed. He couldn't tell her those things. He couldn't bear to see the look of utter disgust on her face.

Drawing in a deep breath, he said, "Years ago, I was different, Callie. But growing up changes a person."

"Growing up. Is that what you call it?" she asked softly.

He turned his gaze back to hers. "What would you call it?"

"Living through a tragedy."

Yes, he'd lived through a tragedy, Tyler thought. Callie just didn't know that the heartbreak had started for him long before Luanne died.

He shifted around so that he was facing her and ran his fingers through her silky hair. "Oh, Callie, I want you to know that I've laughed and smiled more since I met you than I have in a long, long time."

Her brown eyes were glowing as she linked

her hands at the back of his neck and pulled him toward her. "I'm glad, Tyler. I want to think I've given you some happiness. Because you've given me that and so much more."

Her words swelled his chest with emotions that were so raw and real they sent fingers of fear crawling down his spine. In an effort to ignore them, he closed the gap between their lips and kissed her thoroughly. But even though the taste of her filled him with desire, the pressure in his chest was still there.

Why did he want to pull Callie into his arms and simply hold her until the warmth of her body melded with his? Until the fear of loving and losing was pushed completely out of his mind?

"Callie, I can't get enough of you," he whispered against her lips. "Tell me you're not getting tired of me. Of this."

Groaning, she slipped her arms around his neck and scooted closer so that the front of her body was pressing into his.

"Never, Tyler. I'll never get tired of us being together." She brushed a light kiss against his lips, then stood and reached for his hand. "I don't think it's too early to go to bed, do you?"

He rose, then bending at the knees, picked her up and cradled her against his chest. "Not a bit too early. We need our rest."

The bedroom was only illuminated by a night-light near Maeve's crib, but the glow was enough for him to see his way to the side of the bed.

After he'd set Callie on her feet, he went to lock the door, then returned to her side and began to slowly and methodically remove her clothing.

Something was different with him tonight, he realized as his hands slipped over her smooth, creamy skin. The desperate urge to relieve the sexual tension inside him had undergone some sort of transformation. The need to be inside her warm body, to experience the give-and-take between them, was still there, burning in his loins, but there was something else, too. Something precious and tender was working its way right to his heart.

Momentarily stunned by the feeling, he paused, his hands on her shoulders, to rest his cheek against the top of her head.

"Tyler? Is something wrong?"

No. Yes. Oh hell, he didn't know anymore. How could a man want to hold on to something so tightly, while, in the back of his mind, wanted to run as fast and as far as he could? He was having a breakdown, he decided. And he didn't have a clue how to stop it.

Chapter Nine

"Everything is okay, Callie," he told her. "I just feel like holding you—slowing down and enjoying this time we're together. Is that okay with you?"

She tilted her head back and in the semi-darkness he could see moisture sparkling in her brown eyes.

"It's perfect with me," she whispered.

He placed a kiss on her lips before he removed the last of her clothing and started on his.

While he finished the task, Callie folded

back the covers on the bed and they climbed in together.

Tyler pulled her into his arms and she pillowed her head on his shoulder. As they lay quietly in the dark room, he could hear the faint sounds of traffic in the distance, then a dog's bark followed by the high-pitched voice of a child.

Before tonight, he hadn't noticed the muted sounds of town outside the apartment. But that was probably because he'd always been too honed in on Callie and the urgent need to make love to her. He had not heard anything other than her soft breaths and his own heartbeat pounding in his ears.

But now, with a moment to ponder, he was remembering summer nights on the ranch when he'd lain in bed listening to the singing crickets and frogs, the call of night birds, and the howling of coyotes. The Flying A was where he truly belonged and he had a feeling that Callie understood that much about him.

What would happen if he tried to fit Callie into his life on the ranch? She wasn't the sort to crave bright lights and excitement. But that didn't mean she'd be content to live in the country with nothing around her but cows and horses, and him and Maeve. It hadn't been enough for Luanne. How could he expect it to keep Callie happy?

These nights he was spending in her apartment were only temporary, and the more he looked forward, the more he could see the crossroads ahead. He was going to have to make a choice about Callie. He wanted what was best for her, for him and, most of all, for Maeve. His daughter had already lost her mother. If things didn't work out with Callie, she'd be losing another one.

The sober thoughts circling in his head were suddenly interrupted by the movement of Callie's hand sliding gently across the middle of his chest.

"I had lunch with my mother today," she said. "And you know what I was thinking as I sat across from her?"

"Hmm. Probably how blessed you were to have a mother. One who cares about you."

She said, "That thought is always with me. But today I was noticing exactly how beautiful she is. You've not met her, but if you did, you'd agree with me. She's tall, blond, and her eyes are the color of the sky."

His forefinger gently stroked her cheek. "Well, her daughter has beautiful brown eyes and sable colored hair that shines like a piece of satin."

The corners of her lips tilted into a smile. "Thank you for the compliment, Tyler."

"My pleasure."

She said, "To be honest, I never got any special praise from my past boyfriends. Guess their egos were too big to tell a girl she was pretty or smart."

"Hmm. Just how many boyfriends have you had?"

"Only two serious boyfriends. Before that I only had a few casual dates. The ones I believed were serious both walked out on me. For a while I asked myself what I'd done wrong to make them end things with me. But now that I've grown older and wiser, I realize I didn't do anything wrong. Each of them had commitment issues. The kind I couldn't fix. But that's okay, because I figure when I find the right man he'll want to stick around and love me just for me."

Yes, Callie deserved that much from a man and so much more, Tyler thought.

With a forefinger beneath her chin, he tilted her face up to his. "Listen, sweetheart, you deserve every compliment I give you and more."

"Tyler, you don't have to say those things. As long as you're here next to me, that's enough."

Enough for how long?

Tyler didn't let the question linger in his thoughts. He lowered his lips to hers and let the sweetness of her kiss carry him away to a place where there were no doubts or fears.

When he finally pulled his mouth from hers, he planted a row of kisses along her jawline then down the side of her neck. Eventually, he closed his lips around one rosy-brown nipple and teased the bud with his tongue. She reacted by twining her legs around his and pressing her hands against his buttocks.

"Tyler, I want you. So much. More than you can feel. More than I can tell you."

Her voice was thick with passion and the sound of it dialed the heat in his loins to an even higher level. The need to be inside her, to feel her velvety softness surround him, was rapidly turning into an unbearable ache.

"I'm on fire for you, sweetheart," he whispered huskily as he untangled himself from her embrace. "Let me get the protection."

He left the bed long enough to roll on the condom, but when he returned to the mattress to position himself over her, she was quick to place a hand on his shoulder and push him flat against his back.

"It's my turn on top this time," she whispered as she quickly straddled him.

Entranced by this new, cheeky attitude, he planted his hands on either side of her waist and guided her onto his hard erection until there was nothing left to give her.

"Oh, Ty. This is too good." Her raspy words were disrupted with groans of pleasure. "You're too good."

"No, Callie. I'm nothing without you."

He pulled her mouth to his and sensations slammed him from all directions as her hips began to move against him and her hands skimmed over his heated skin. All thoughts of tomorrow and the crossroads ahead were suddenly and completely wiped from his mind. All that he could think was that Callie was taking him to places he'd never been before and he didn't want the journey to end.

It was long after midnight when they finished making love a second time. By then, both were spent and close to falling asleep.

With Callie's warm body spooned against his, he nuzzled her silky hair and closed his eyes. The alarm on the nightstand was set for five. Hardly enough sleep. But even jumping out of bed at five still made it a race to make it to the ranch in time to get Maeve situated with his mother and meet up with his father and brothers.

Pressing a kiss to the edge of her temple, he said, "You're ruining me, Callie girl. You're making it harder and harder for me to leave your bed in the mornings."

"Mmm. I wish we could stay here for days."

Days? Weeks or months? Would that be enough to satiate his desire for her?

"Days might kill me," he told her.

She didn't reply and from the steady, even sound of her breathing, he realized she was falling asleep.

"We'll sleep tomorrow night," she murmured drowsily.

He stroked his fingers through her hair, wondering how many tomorrow nights they would have before something ripped them apart.

Shutting his mind to the question, he whispered, "Good night, Callie."

"Good night, my love."

For a few seconds, Tyler wasn't sure what he'd heard and he stared down at her in a trance of wonder and unease. Had she really called him her love? Had her feelings for him grown that deeply?

What about your feelings for Callie? Have you done the unthinkable and fallen in love with her?

Icy fear washed over him and his first instinct was to leap from the bed and get out of the apartment as fast as his legs could carry him. But he couldn't do that just yet. He couldn't chance moving around the room and waking Callie. No, he'd sneak out later, after she'd fallen into a deep sleep. That way he wouldn't have to admit to her face that he was a sniveling coward.

Instead of being roused by the buzzing sound of the alarm before daylight, Callie opened her eyes to sunlight streaming through the window and the digital numbers on the clock reading six forty-five.

Oh! What happened to the alarm?

She flipped over to find Tyler's side of the

bed empty. That fact had her bounding off the mattress and racing over to Maeve's crib.

The baby wasn't there.

Confused and just a little worried, Callie hurried out to the kitchen. Before he left in the mornings, Tyler always made coffee and filled his vacuum cup to drink on the drive to the Flying A. But there was no coffee in the machine, nor was there a sign that any had been made earlier this morning.

And then she saw the simple note tacked to the refrigerator with a heart-shaped magnet.

Had to leave. Talk soon.

Dumbfounded by the short message, she stared at the small scrap of paper. Had an accident occurred with his family? Had Maeve become ill in the night and he hadn't wanted to wake Callie?

No. That didn't make sense. Something else was going on with Tyler to send him driving off without a word to her.

Feeling sick to her stomach, Callie tossed the note into the waste bin and hurried to the bathroom. She didn't have time to figure it out now. She had to get ready for work. Later today, if she didn't hear from Tyler, she'd contact him.

Time crawled by for Callie. Even though Bronco Ghost Tours had a steady stream of customers throughout the day, she found herself constantly checking her phone for a text or a missed call from Tyler.

By four o'clock, still with no word from him, she told Saundra she was taking a little break and carried her phone outside to the back of the building.

She prepared something in her head to leave on his voice mail. She was taken by surprise when he answered on the second ring.

"Tyler! Oh, I'm so relieved to hear your voice. I was afraid something had happened to Maeve or to you, or someone in your family."

There was a pause and then he said, "I'm sorry. I didn't mean for you to worry."

The sick feeling swimming in Callie's stomach all day suddenly intensified to a burning knot.

"I couldn't imagine why you left without waking me."

"I knew you were tired," he said. "I wanted to let you sleep."

She didn't believe him. Not for one minute. There was a distant, strained sound to his voice. It was something she'd never heard from him before.

"Okay. Well, that was thoughtful of you—only I much rather you had said goodbye in person."

In the background, she heard Maeve let out a squeal followed by the sound of banging. The baby was probably pounding her teething ring on the tray of a high chair, Callie thought. And the sudden urge to see the little girl, to hold her in her arms, caused her throat to tighten.

When he didn't immediately reply, she said, "I hear Maeve. I'm sorry, I should have asked you if you were busy. I can call back later."

"No. I'm not that busy. We finished up early today. I'm about to feed Maeve a little snack."

"Oh. Should I expect to see you later then? I still have about an hour and a half of work here at the office."

Silence stretched for so long that Callie pulled the phone away from her ear to glance at the screen just to make sure the signal hadn't died.

"No. I can't make it tonight, Callie."

Callie glanced around her, but she wasn't seeing anything in the quiet alleyway that ran behind the Ghost Tours' building. Neither did she notice the clouds drifting overhead. Or feel the warm breeze that brushed her face and hair.

Tyler was ending things. For some reason that she couldn't begin to fathom, he had decided to put an end to their time together.

All the guys I've ever seriously dated ended things with me.

The words she'd spoken to Tyler last night as they'd lain in bed came back to her now and the irony very nearly made her burst out laughing. Except that she couldn't laugh. Not when her heart was splitting down the middle.

"If I was a nice girl, I'd say I understand," she said crisply. "But at this moment I'm not feeling too nice. And I don't understand. Are you needed at the ranch tonight? Something to do with your family?"

Another pause and then he said, "No, Callie. I—I'm sorry. I get that I'm not doing this well—at all. But I don't know how to say this. Except that things with us are moving too fast for me. I believe it would be best if we didn't see each other for a while. I need some time and space to figure out what all this means for both of us."

Space. Time. Who was he trying to fool? Why didn't he have the guts to simply spit out the way he really felt and tell her it was over?

She wanted to fling the question at him. She wanted to tell him he should have the decency to make a clean break of things. Not keep her dangling. But she couldn't force the words past her aching throat.

Idiot that she was, she loved him. And the vulnerable part of her heart wanted to believe a span of time away from her might be what he needed to realize they belonged together.

"Callie? Are you still there?"

His voice jerked her back to reality and she swallowed hard and spoke in the most benevolent voice she could muster. "Yes, I'm here. You're perfectly right, Tyler. You need time. I do, too. It's been fun. But I remember you saying that fun isn't your thing and—"

"Callie, I—"

She interrupted, using the same charitable tone as before. "No, Tyler. I'm perfectly okay with your decision. I only ask one thing of you. Give Maeve a hug and kiss for me."

"Sure. I will."

She disconnected the call and pulled in several deep breaths before finally managing to compose herself enough to enter the building.

Halfway down the hall to her office, she met Saundra hurrying toward her. "I was coming after you. I need…" She paused and peered at Callie's strained face. "Callie! What in heck is wrong? Pardon the pun, but you look like you've seen a ghost."

"Funny you should say that, Saundra. I just now encountered a real one. And you know what I discovered? You can't fight a ghost. Don't even try, because you'll lose."

Tyler carried Maeve into his parents' kitchen and set the baby on an open area of the floor. His daughter promptly took off in a rapid crawl to her grandmother, who was standing at the sink washing up the last of the pots and pans she'd used to cook dinner.

Hannah bent and spent a moment chitchatting baby talk to her granddaughter before she straightened and looked over to where Tyler had taken a chair at the kitchen table.

"What are you doing in here? You're supposed to be in the living room with your father and brothers. Hutch wants all of his sons' opinions about investing in more land. That includes you, Tyler."

"I've already discussed the deal with Dad. Whatever he and my brothers decide is okay with me. Land is always a good investment. And we could use more grazing land. Plus, the price is right."

Hannah dried a saucepan and stored it away in the cabinet. "It's good that you agree with your father. But it's not often all five of you are together at the same time. I thought you'd be in there enjoying their company."

This evening Hannah had prepared a big meal of roast beef and all the trimmings for her husband and five sons. Normally, Tyler loved anything his mother cooked, but he'd had to force himself to eat a respectable portion of the food on his plate. And Tyler always enjoyed the camaraderie he shared with his father and brothers, but tonight he'd struggled to participate. His mind had kept drifting, making it impossible to focus on what any of them was saying about cattle and land, and the prospect of expanding the Flying A.

A whole week had passed since he'd crept from Callie's apartment like a thief not wanting to get caught with the goods. And he felt no better about himself now than he had that night.

No matter what he was doing, or how loud the noises around him, nothing could drown out the sound of Callie's voice when she'd called him that next afternoon. He had not been expecting to hear from her so soon. Actually, he'd figured after she'd read his note and found him and Maeve gone, she'd be too peeved to speak to him for a few days at least. Her call had caught him off guard and he'd struggled to find anything to say that made sense.

Not that catching him off guard was an excuse, he thought grimly. Even if he'd been given weeks to prepare a speech in his defense, he would've still floundered like a babbling fool.

My love. How could he explain that merely

hearing her murmur those words as she'd fallen asleep had frozen him with fear? All the years of hurt and disappointments with Luanne had suddenly slapped him in the face. Oh yes, his wife had once said she loved him, too. But after living on the ranch for a while, she'd decided love wasn't nearly as rosy and wonderful as she'd expected it to be. Whatever she'd felt for him had turned to stone and she'd viewed living with him on the Flying A the same as being jailed. So the idea of trusting his heart to another woman was worse than walking on the edge of a cliff after dark.

A heavy breath eased past his lips. "I see that hairy-legged bunch every day, Mom. You're much better company than they are."

"You didn't think so when I made you sit at that very table and do your homework," she said with a chuckle.

After drying her hands on a dishtowel, Hannah moved to the end of the countertop and poured two cups of coffee from a glass carafe. But before she could carry them over to the table, Maeve grabbed her by the ankle and whimpered loudly.

"What's the matter, little darlin'? You want Grandma to hold you?"

She picked up the baby, but as soon as she settled Maeve on one hip, the girl went as stiff as a board and cried louder.

"Put her back down, Mom. She's been cranky these past few days. She doesn't know what she wants."

Hannah placed Maeve on the floor and handed the baby two aluminum pie plates to play with. "Maybe that will keep you occupied for a minute or two," she said to her granddaughter.

With Maeve momentarily pacified with the pans, Hannah carried the coffee, along with creamer and sugar, over to the table and set one of the cups in front of Tyler. "Here," she said, "have another cup. Would you like more cobbler? There's plenty left over."

"No thanks, Mom. I'm full to the brim. Everything was really good." He spooned creamer and sugar into the cup and stirred.

"But you shouldn't have gone to all the trouble of cooking such a big meal."

"Nonsense. This was an everyday chore while you boys were growing up. I actually miss it."

Other than working occasionally as a substitute teacher at the elementary school in town, Hannah had always been a rancher's wife. Along with taking care of her family, she also helped out with some of the chores around the ranch. She enjoyed the country life as much as Hutch, and Tyler had often thought how lucky his parents were to be so compatible. Or did a couple have to be like-minded to be happy? he wondered. Maybe they just needed to be truly and deeply in love like Hannah and Hutch.

"Mom, you're one in a million."

Smiling wanly, she said, "You're a bit biased, honey. I'm not any different than a million other women."

"You'll never make me believe that."

While he sipped his coffee, Hannah regarded him thoughtfully.

After a moment, she said, "I should probably tell you that Dean is very worried about you."

Tyler bit back a curse. "Would you tell me why Dean feels like it's his job to keep his nose stuck in my life?" he asked crossly. "You'd think I was his son instead of his little brother!"

His outburst caused Hannah to stare at him. "Sorry. Guess I hit a sore spot."

Tyler heaved out a heavy breath then wearily pinched the bridge of his nose. "No, I'm the one who's sorry, Mom. I didn't mean to burst out like that. It's just that Dean is always trying to tell me what and what not to do."

"Isn't that usually what big brothers do?"

"Up to a point. But Garrett, Weston and Crosby are my older brothers, too, and they don't treat me like Dean does," Tyler pointed out.

Hannah reached over and rested a hand on Tyler's forearm. "I'm not sure if your father or I ever mentioned this before, but when I got pregnant with you, Dean was ecstatic. Having three brothers already, he wanted a little sister so badly. That's all he could talk about. And then when you turned out to be a boy, we just knew Dean was going to be devastated."

This was something he hadn't heard before and the idea of a six-year-old Dean longing for a sister was difficult for Tyler to imagine.

"What did he do?" Tyler asked. "Pout for a week?"

She smiled with fond remembrance. "Are you kidding? He was over the moon. From that day on, he was like a little mother hen with you. And while you were growing up, I never had to worry as much about you, because I knew Dean was always going to be watching and making sure you didn't get hurt." She patted his arm. "Have patience with him, Ty. When he sticks his nose in, it's because he loves you."

Just hearing how much Dean had always loved him made Tyler feel even more like the dirt on the bottom of his boot.

"Yeah, I get that, Mom. I've been…dealing with a lot of things right now. That's all."

"Dean sees that you're suffering. And I see it, too. It's Callie, isn't it?" she asked gently.

Watching Maeve sitting in the middle of the kitchen floor, crashing the two aluminum plates together like orchestra cymbals, had him thinking back to the first night he'd met Callie. She'd been so distant with his daughter that he'd drawn the conclusion she disliked babies altogether. And then it turned out she'd actually felt like Tyler had when Maeve had been born. Afraid and inept.

But Callie's fears of baby care had quickly evaporated and, after a short amount of time, she'd been changing Maeve's diaper and feeding her as if she'd done it for years. Watching the two of them together had been almost like watching a mother with her baby daughter.

Was Maeve missing Callie? Was that why she'd been so cranky these past few days? Tyler hated to think so. He also hated to think that Callie might be missing the baby. But, damn it, that wasn't his fault.

When a man made a mistake, he was supposed to learn from it. And God knows he'd made plenty with Luanne. Now he was trying to be sensible. He was trying to avoid more pain and heartache in the future. In the meantime, how was he supposed to deal with the empty ache gnawing inside him?

"What happened?" Hannah persisted. "Was Maeve too much for her? You need to understand that it's sometimes hard for a woman to step into a ready-made family."

His mother's questions were like sharp darts to his heart. "No. Callie loved Maeve— she adored her. It's nothing like that, Mom." He grimaced as he forced himself to face his mother's inquisitive gaze. "You should know by now that the problem is me. I'm the one who's a twisted, emotional wreck of a man."

"Tyler—"

"It's true, Mom. I made a mess of my marriage. I never really talked all that much about it to you and Dad. Frankly, because

I was ashamed for either of you to know how it really was. But I'll admit now—it was painful. I couldn't be what Luanne needed and I guess she couldn't be what I wanted." He wiped a hand over his face. "When I met Callie, it was all so different. She was sweet and understanding. She never made demands. All she ever did was be good to me."

"Maybe Callie smothered you?"

"If I accused her of that, I'd be a heel and a liar. I was the one who did all the smothering. And then, all of a sudden, a few days ago, I realized if I didn't put a stop to things I was going to— Well, get too serious."

"You mean like fall in love with her?" she asked knowingly.

Thank God this was his mother he was talking to. Anybody else and he would've already walked out of the room.

"Yeah. Something like that," he admitted on a long, weary breath. "I ended up telling her that I believed it would be best if we didn't see each other."

"And is it? Best?" she asked gently. "What's so bad about falling in love with Callie? Think about it, Ty. Without love, life is damned empty."

Tyler rarely heard his mother utter a curse word and that was only when she was exasperated. He was staring at her when Maeve grabbed onto his leg and pulled herself to her feet.

The baby was a pleasurable distraction and he affectionately ruffled the top of her sandy-blond curls. "Hi, sweetie. Want to show Grandma how you can walk?"

"She can walk?" Hannah asked with surprise. "I haven't heard about this!"

"Well, she's not exactly walking. But she's getting close to it." Tyler reached for the baby's hand, but Maeve shrugged it off and turned away from his leg that she'd been using as a leaning post.

"Goo-da-deee!" the baby cried out. Before Tyler could grab her, she took a step forward. Then another and another.

"Oh! Look at that! She's walking, Ty!" Hannah shouted with happy excitement.

Maeve took two more steps before her balance teetered and her bottom plopped onto the tiled floor.

The baby looked around in surprise. "Gaga-gee!"

Hannah laughed. "I think she's shocked herself."

"She shocked me a little, too," Tyler said. "I didn't expect her to take off like that."

Leaving his seat, Tyler plucked the baby off the floor and smacked several kisses on her cheek.

"What a girl!" he exclaimed. "Let's see if you can do it again."

He stood her on the floor and holding on to one hand, urged her to step forward. But she instantly balked and let out an annoyed cry.

Hannah laughed. "Five steps are more than enough for her right now, Daddy. She has her own ideas about when she wants to walk."

"She has her own ideas about everything."

He set Maeve back on the floor and she went crawling across the tile to fetch the pie pans.

He returned to his chair at the table, thinking how much he'd like to pull out his phone and share the news with Callie. She'd taken such delight in trying to help Maeve walk. She'd be thrilled to hear the baby had finally succeeded to take a few solo steps.

But he couldn't let himself phone her. No. Once he heard her voice, he'd be lost. He'd be asking to see her again. And if she agreed, then he'd be right back where he'd been. In her arms and treading on thin ice—just as his brother had warned.

"Hey, what's going on in here?" Dean questioned as he strode into the kitchen. "Mom, I could hear you all the way out to the living room."

Rising from the chair, Hannah gleefully clapped her hands together. "We just had a big moment in here. My darling little granddaughter was walking!"

Dean looked over to where Maeve was sitting on the floor waving one of the pie pans in the air. "Maeve walked? Oh boy! Now Ty will really have his work cut out for him. He'll be chasing Maeve all over the place. And look at him. He's already a pile of bones!"

Tyler couldn't deny that he'd lost weight since his break with Callie, so he didn't bother to contradict Dean's remark. Learning that his brother had always viewed himself as Tyler's little daddy had changed how he viewed Dean's overprotective attitude.

"Okay, Dean," Tyler said amiably. "Now that Maeve is on the verge of racing around the house, I'll eat another helping of Mom's cobbler."

"Good. Make it a big dish," Dean told him. Crossing over to his niece, he scooped her up in his arms and bounced her until she squealed with delight.

While Dean carried Maeve around the kitchen, Hannah stepped up behind Tyler and gently patted his shoulder.

"Maeve is growing, son, and I'd like to think you are, too," she said in a voice meant only for his ears. "That part about you being a twisted mess is wrong. And I believe Callie would be the first one to tell you so."

Reaching up, he gave her hand a grateful squeeze and then rose from the chair. "I'd better get that cobbler before Dean decides to force feed me."

The hour was late when the family gathering at the main ranch house broke up and Tyler made the short drive home. Maeve was still awake when he changed her clothes for a onesie, but as soon as he placed her in her crib, she closed her eyes and immediately grew quiet.

Tyler's day had been spent with Weston and Crosby, building more than a mile of new fence, along with a trip to Bronco Feed and Ranch Supply in town for a load of cedar post and several rolls of barbed wire. The dinner at his parents had added to the long day. Exhaustion had finally caught up to him and his movements felt laden with lead as he slowly slipped off his shirt and walked over to the king-size bed that monopolized one end of the large bedroom.

This morning, before he'd left the house, he had not bothered to straighten the covers. Now, as he smoothed the sheet and comforter and punched the pillow back to life, he couldn't help but think about Callie's warm bed. The way the sheets had always smelled like her and the way she'd used his shoulder for a pillow rather than the down-filled one.

Forsaking the idea of sleep, Tyler raked both hands through his tousled hair and walked out to the den. He turned on the small TV in the corner and, after scrolling through several channels and finding nothing garnering his attention, he cursed, turned it off, and tossed the remote onto the couch.

Damn it! Why couldn't he count the blessings he had, instead of dwelling on all that he'd lost? He had loving, supportive parents and brothers, a successful ranch, and, most especially, he had a beautiful little daughter.

He'd been full of pride as he'd watched Maeve take her first steps. But his joy and pride had been dampened when he'd thought about Callie and how much joy she would've gotten from seeing Maeve reach an important milestone.

His mother, who was more perceptive than any person had a right to be, had instinctively known what was going through his mind. She'd understood how empty and lost he'd been feeling. Yet in spite of all that, she fully expected him to grow stronger from all the adversity he'd gone through. She wanted him to find the courage to love again.

What his mother, or anyone else, didn't understand was that Tyler had no right to be in love and to be happy. He didn't even have the right to be alive. He was the one who should've been killed. Not Luanne.

He began to pace the length of the long room as questions slammed him left and right. How the hell was he supposed to have any kind of life with a woman? How could he expect to make Callie happy? His heart was carrying around a ton of guilt and remorse. How could he make room in it for love? The kind of love that Callie deserved?

Tell me more about the house. Does it have a fireplace?

Callie's question managed to push through the misery in his mind and, with his jaw clamped against the pain, he walked over to the huge rock fireplace that stretched across the end of the room.

On the mantel there was a photo of Luanne and himself on their wedding day. And another of her sitting on one of the ranch's horses. In the latter, she was wearing a smile, but the expression hadn't been genuine. She'd not wanted to be on the horse in the first place. Tyler had begged and cajoled until she'd eventually given in and climbed into the saddle long enough for him to snap a photo. She'd given in to his wishes reluctantly. Just like she'd lived here on the ranch for the last five and a half years of her life.

His jaw set, he slipped off his wedding band, then pulled the two photos off the mantel and walked through the house removing everything that was remotely connected to his late wife. After packing the items into a box, he carried it to the attic and stacked it with other containers of memorabilia he hadn't had the heart to throw away.

For his daughter's sake, he'd left a photo of Luanne in Maeve's room. And someday when Maeve was old enough to understand, he'd show everything to her. But until then, the memories needed to remain packed away.

As he turned out the attic light and climbed down the ladder, a sense of relief came over him and he realized he should've found the courage to do this months ago. But he'd wanted to keep things as they were, to let himself believe that Luanne wasn't really gone. That he wasn't going to be raising their daughter alone.

He wasn't sure what had changed in him tonight. But he'd finally come to the eye-opening conclusion that Luanne had never thought of this house as her home. And now that he looked back on their marriage, he wasn't all that sure she'd ever actually considered him her husband.

Chapter Ten

"Saundra, I'm going to Bronco Java and Juice. Want to come along?" Callie asked her coworker as she shouldered her handbag and walked toward the front entrance. "Evan is out, but Josh is in the back going over the details of a new tour. He'll watch the front for us."

Saundra turned away from the display window where she'd been pulling a black T-shirt with a ghost figure onto a headless mannequin.

"Oh, thanks for asking, Callie, but I actually have a lunch date a little later today."

This was the first Callie had heard about it. How had Saundra kept this kind of news to herself?

"A date? Good for you! Do I know him?"

Grinning, Saundra walked over to Callie. "I don't think so. He works at Rapid-Ship down the street. I see him whenever I take merchandise down there to be shipped out to customers. One day we started talking and the more we talked, the better things got. He likes redheads," she added with a sly wink.

"Lucky you. I hope it works out."

"Well, I do, too. At least for a couple of dates," she said with a chuckle. Her expression sobered as she studied Callie's pale face. "What about you, honey? I've not asked in a couple of days, but have you heard anything from Tyler?"

Callie's head swung glumly back and forth. "No. And to tell you the truth, Saundra, I don't believe I will. He's obviously not interested in me anymore."

Just saying that out loud was painful, but Callie was getting used to the constant ache in her chest. She only wondered how many more days or weeks needed to pass before she started to feel like a human being again.

"Callie, I find it hard to believe that Tyler turned out to be such a cad. I thought…well, never mind what I thought. You better go on to lunch. I'll hold down the fort until you get back."

"Thanks, Saundra."

Because the day was full of bright sunshine, Callie purposely chose to walk the distance to Bronco Java and Juice in the hope that the fresh air would lift her spirits. On the way, she admitted to herself that she was filled with anticipation at a chance encounter with Tyler and Maeve. In fact, she'd visited the place twice last week with the same thought in mind, but Tyler had never showed. In fact, one of the waitresses had stopped by her table and inquired about Tyler. She'd told Callie they hadn't seen him and the baby in a long while.

She could only hope today would be different, Callie thought as she entered the sunny coffee and juice bar. Today Tyler might accidently be in town and decide to eat lunch before he headed back to the ranch.

After taking a small table at the back of the dining area, a waitress came and took her order for a juice drink and a pimento cheese sandwich. Since it was only eleven thirty, the place wasn't full yet, but more people were steadily arriving and, each time the bell over the door tinkled, Callie looked up, hoping to see Tyler.

"Hi, Callie. Good to see you today. Have you been waited on?"

Callie pulled her eyes from the door to see Cassidy Ware standing beside her table. Dressed in jeans and a T-shirt, her long blond hair pulled into a ponytail, she looked more like a fresh-faced teenager than the owner of a booming restaurant.

"Oh hi, Cassidy! Yes, a waitress has already taken my order." Callie gestured to one of the empty chairs. "I'd love for you to join me for a minute. That is, if you're not too busy."

Smiling, Cassidy pulled out one of the chairs and sank into it. "The lunch hour is just getting started. But I'll take a minute anyway," she said. "We've already had a monstrous morning. I could use a cup of coffee myself right now."

"I don't have to ask you how business is doing," Callie said. "I can see for myself that the place is always jammed full. Do you ever think about expanding?"

"I wish. But there's just no place here to expand. A street runs in front and behind the building. And the businesses I'm sandwiched between have no plans to ever move. I could move to another location, but I love this one. Still, you know what they say, never say never."

A waitress arrived with Callie's order and she'd thoughtfully brought her boss a cup of fresh coffee.

"Thanks, Teresa. I'll give you a tip for this," Cassidy told the woman.

Callie began to eat as Cassidy said, "I've

noticed a few ghost tours around town after dark. You guys must be staying busy, too."

"We are. Evan is constantly coming up with ideas for different tours and bringing in fresh merchandise. We all stay very busy." A fact that Callie appreciated. She didn't want extra time to sit around and dwell on how happy being with Tyler had made her. And how utterly miserable she was without him.

Cassidy sipped her coffee. "Well, it looks like Bronco is going to get even busier when November rolls around. It's been announced that the Mistletoe Rodeo is a go. And with the competition being a two-week long affair, there should be hordes of people flooding into Bronco. Especially with Geoff Burris coming back to host the whole thing. You know he's a big rodeo star, don't you?"

"Rodeo star? Uh, yes, I've heard he's very successful," Callie answered. "I'm sure Bronco will be hopping once he arrives."

Did Tyler like rodeo competitions? Callie wondered. Since he spent many of his days roping and riding on the ranch, he probably knew all about the sport. Still, she couldn't picture him doing something as festive as going to a rodeo.

"Yoo-hoo, Callie. Are you with me?"

Realizing she'd missed part of what Cassidy had been saying, she quickly apologized. "Sorry, Cassidy, I was thinking about something."

"Clearly." She peered closer at Callie's face. "As soon as I sat down here, I had the feeling that something was wrong. What is it?"

Callie blew out a long breath and placed her half-eaten sandwich back on the plate. "It's very easy to explain, Cassidy. I've been a complete idiot. I've fallen for a man whose heart still belongs to his dead wife."

Cassidy studied her for a brief moment then leaned her head closer so that no one else could overhear. "If you're talking about Tyler, then I think you have it all wrong, Callie."

Confused by the woman's remark, she asked, "What do you mean? Wrong about what?"

"About Tyler's feelings for his wife. From what I saw of them when they were out together, I suspect their marriage was on the rocks long before she died. I even heard rumors from friends that all was not well in that Abernathy household."

Callie was stunned. If this was true, maybe she'd just learned the reason why Tyler had never mentioned his wife or talked about their life together. Maybe he hadn't wanted Callie to know that his marriage had been failing.

"I thought— All this time I believed Tyler was madly in love with Luanne."

"If he was, he hid it well," Cassidy said, adding with an encouraging smile, "If you really care that much for the guy, I wouldn't give up on him. I'd put up a fight."

Callie had never fought for a man's affections. Up until Tyler, she'd never had one worth fighting for. "I'm not sure I'd know how to do that, Cassidy. Especially when I think Tyler is hiding from me—maybe even from life in general."

"Then you have to root him out. Make him face you and whatever else that's making him hide."

Callie was mulling over Cassidy's advice when the barking of a dog caught her attention. Both women looked in the direction of the sound, which seemed to be coming from somewhere in the back of the building.

"Oh, I guess Scooter's here. That's what I call him. He shows up every now and then and scratches at the back door, begging for scraps. I've called animal control, but so far they've never been able to catch the little scamp."

"A stray dog? Is it white with a brown eye patch?" Callie asked.

Cassidy frowned thoughtfully. "The dog is white, but I don't recall about the brown patch. Why? Does he belong to you?"

Callie shook her head. "One of Daphne's dogs at Happy Hearts has gone missing. I was just wondering if your stray might be her dog."

"Oh, I'll go see. If Scooter fits the description, I'll contact Daphne." She quickly rose from the table. "See you later, Callie."

Cassidy left for the kitchen and Callie took a few final sips of juice before she picked up her check and headed to the counter to pay. Her lunch hour was nearly over and it was obvious Tyler wasn't going to show.

The sensible thing for her to do would be to forget the man, Callie told herself as she walked back to work. Yet she still couldn't shake the feeling that he needed her in some way. And now that Cassidy had hinted that his marriage might have been in shambles, the feeling had intensified.

But what good was that going to do? she asked herself. Even if Tyler's heart wasn't pining for his late wife, he obviously didn't want to be with Callie. And the fact was crushing her.

"Van, you're going to have to tell everyone at the wedding that I woke up sick this morning and I couldn't make it to the ceremony."

Vanessa glanced away from the dresser

mirror where she was applying mascara to her already long lashes and stared at Callie, who was standing in the bedroom doorway.

"I am not going to lie for you, Callie Sheldrick. You're not sick. You're being a big coward!"

Callie's shoulders slumped in resignation. "Okay, I admit it. I am a coward. We both know that Tyler will be there to see Gabe exchange vows with Mel."

"Not just Tyler. I'm sure every branch of the Abernathy family will be in attendance. If you happen to be in the right place at the right time, you might even get a chance to meet Tyler's parents."

"Oh no. I'm not about to try to insinuate myself in his family. Tyler is a very private person. Besides, you're forgetting the fact that he's made it painfully clear I'm no longer a part of his life."

Vanessa pushed the wand back into the mascara tube and walked over to Callie. "When you talked to him last, did he tell you those exact words?"

"No. But I'm not stupid, Van. There is such a thing as common deduction. I've not heard a peep from the guy. He doesn't have to shout the words from a rooftop for me to get the message. And now you expect me to go to Mel's wedding and pretend that I'm not—"

"You're not what?" Vanessa gently prompted.

Callie couldn't stop the tears she'd been trying to hold back. They spilled onto her cheeks. "Dying inside," she finally managed to say.

"Oh, Callie, honey." Vanessa gently curved an arm around her shoulders. "I understand that you've had some disappointments when it comes to your love life. But you need to believe that things will eventually turn out as they should."

Callie sniffed and tried to smile. "You mean if Tyler is meant to be my soul mate then it will magically happen? Dear Lord, I'm getting worried about you, Van. You're sounding more like your great-grandmother Winona every day."

Grinning, Vanessa gave Callie's shoulders a squeeze. "Now you're sounding more like my happy little Callie." She turned her around and gave her a nudge to her bedroom across the hall. "Go get dressed and make yourself beautiful. And if it will make you feel any better, you can ride with me and Jameson to the wedding."

"Not on your life. You two lovebirds need to take in this wedding atmosphere all alone. Thanks for the offer, but I'll drive myself."

"All right. But don't think you're going to back out. If I don't spot you in the crowd, I'm driving back here to the apartment to get you."

Sighing, Callie shook her head. "Don't worry. I'll be there. And I'll try to put a smile on my face."

Tyler had rather shovel manure out of ten horse stalls than go to Gabe's wedding. But all the Abernathys would be there and it would look worse than strange if Tyler didn't show up for the big event. Besides, if he'd tried to hide away on the ranch, Dean would've roped, tied, and dragged him to the ceremony.

"As far as I'm concerned, this is wasting daylight," Tyler muttered as he stared out the passenger window of Dean's plush pickup. "It would've made more sense for me to be building that last section of fence instead of going to a damned wedding."

"Just relax, Tyler. This shindig will be over before you know it. Anyway, you'll get to have cake and champagne."

"I'd rather have beer."

Dean grunted with amusement. "And pretzels? I doubt Mel chose to serve those two items at the wedding. Now if Gabe had a say, he might've taken pity on us cowboys."

"I'm not worried about eating or drinking," Tyler replied.

The Association, where the wedding and reception was to be held, was a fancy country club for local cattlemen. Joining The Association cost a fortune, but even a large amount of money wasn't enough for a man to acquire membership. A person had to be sponsored by someone who was already a member, so becoming privy to the club's amenities wasn't an easy feat. Tyler would be the first to admit he sometimes enjoyed the finer things in life, but the swanky clubhouse was really not his style. Still, a few years ago, he'd gone through the expense and rigors to become a member because Luanne had urged him to. She'd liked the prestige that came with The Association and had not wanted to miss any of the social functions held at the country club.

Since Luanne's death, Tyler had had no desire or reason to attend the clubhouse. More proof of just how much his life had changed, he thought.

"You might not be worried about the food or drink. But you are worried about running into the little brunette," Dean stated as he braked the truck behind a slower moving car.

"I told you not to call her that. Her name is Callie," Tyler growled at him. "And you're wrong. I'm not worried about seeing her."

"She will be at the wedding, don't you think?"

Think. That's all Tyler had been doing the past few days. Especially since he'd stripped the house of any sign of Luanne.

"I figure nothing less than a dire emergency would keep her away. Mel is her friend."

"That's good."

"What does that mean?"

Dean darted him a frown. "It means you might have a chance to get on your knees and beg her to forgive you."

Tyler's frown matched the one on his brother's face. "Forgive me for what?"

"For starters, running off. Leaving her high and dry."

Tyler bristled. "Who told you something like that? Did Mom—"

Dean held up a hand to halt the rest of his sentence. "Whoa, don't get peeved at Mom. I wrangled the information out of her."

"I should've known. When it comes to me, that nose of yours is pretty damned large."

"I just don't want you to throw away a good thing, brother."

Dean had barely gotten the remark out when The Association clubhouse came into view. Dozens of vehicles were already parked in a designated area away from the massive building. Tyler scanned the assortment of cars and trucks, but he didn't spot Callie's olive-green Jeep.

Maybe she wasn't coming, after all.

A man dressed in a Western suit and black cowboy hat was managing the wedding guest traffic, and Dean followed his directions to an empty space at the end of a long row of vehicles.

Once they were parked and standing outside the truck, Tyler tightened his bolo and tried to tell himself he wouldn't be disappointed if Callie had decided to skip the wedding.

Callie had never seen the outside of The Association clubhouse, much less been inside the elaborate building. But she'd heard about the place. After Jameson had taken Vanessa there for a fancy dinner, she'd given Callie a first-hand description. At the time, she'd thought her roommate had been exaggerating the luxuriousness of the place, but she'd been wrong. If anything, Vanessa had failed to mention many of the lavish details of the natural stone and wood building.

When Callie entered the high-beamed foyer at the front of the building, an usher directed her to a lounge furnished with large leather couches and dark wood tables, illuminated by fancy lamps with beautiful Craftsman-style shades.

Several wedding guests, dressed to the nines, were milling about the massive room and she scanned each group for a sign of a familiar face. When she failed to see one, she moved through an open door that led into another lounge almost a duplicate of the first.

This time, she didn't worry about finding a recognizable face among the people sitting on couches or standing in the small groups chatting and laughing. Instead, Callie practically gawked at the cavernous fireplace with its huge wooden mantel and the massive windows that showcased a majestic scene of tall, jagged mountains in the distance.

Amazed by what she was seeing, Callie wondered if this was how most of the cattlemen of Bronco relaxed. Once, she'd considered asking Tyler if he belonged to The Association, but since he'd never mentioned the club to her, she'd decided against it. Now as she walked from room to room, taking in the elaborate bar area and main dining room, she honestly couldn't see him relaxing in such extravagant surroundings. But then, these past couple of weeks since they'd parted, she'd come to realize that there was a whole lot to Tyler that she didn't know.

"Callie, I was about to think I was going to have to come after you!"

Turning, she saw Vanessa approaching in a rush. Her powder-blue dress skimmed her lush curves while her dark hair was swept to one side to reveal a long, dangling earring of pearls and rhinestones. It was easy to see why Jameson was so smitten with her, Callie thought. She looked incredible.

Callie glanced down at the floral taffeta dress she was wearing. "I couldn't make up my mind about which dress to wear."

"You look lovely." She snatched hold of Callie's arm. "Come on. I think they're about to start seating the guests. You need to sit with me and Jameson."

Vanessa was obviously feeling sorry for Callie because she'd had to attend the wedding without an escort. The idea was humiliating, but it was hardly Callie's main concern. Seeing Tyler again was stretching her nerves to the breaking point.

"This isn't necessary, Van," she insisted as her friend hustled her past the dining area and into another lounge that was packed with guests. On the opposite side of the room, the beautiful notes of a piano drifted through an open doorway. "I'll sit at the back somewhere." Where Tyler might not see her. And she might not see him sitting with the huge

Abernathy family. Yes, that would be better, she thought desperately.

"Don't give me problems. Just enjoy the moment."

By the time they reached the spot where Jameson was waiting, the guests were being ushered into a cavernous room where the ceremony would take place.

Callie tried not to gape in wonder at the fairy-tale sight. Huge baskets of white roses, pink and coral peonies and baby's breath lined the aisle between the endless rows of folding chairs. A trellis covered with the same flowers arched above a wooden altar. Bronze floor candelabras with intricately scrolled holders flanked the altar and lined the outer edges of the seating. The tall candles had already been lit and now the tiny flames gently flickered.

To one side of the room, not far from the altar, a young man dressed in a dark tuxedo was playing a baby grand. Atop the piano sat another huge basket of roses and peonies. Beyond, the massive window exposed a breathtaking view of green and blue mountains in the distance.

The delicate scent of the flowers drifted through the room, along with the poignant notes of a familiar love song. Callie, suddenly struck by the incredibly romantic atmosphere, was forced to blink back tears before she took her seat next to Vanessa.

When she pulled a tissue from her clutch and dabbed at her eyes, Vanessa patted her hand and whispered in her ear. "You're going to be okay, sweetie."

Sure, she'd be okay, Callie thought wryly. Why wouldn't she be? This wasn't the first time a man had broken up with her. Surely she'd survive this one.

But oh, just the thought of one day standing at an altar with Tyler, with flowers and music and their friends and family looking on, was so bittersweet, she could hardly bear it.

She directed a wobbly smile at Vanessa and whispered, "I'm fine. Every woman gets emotional at a wedding, don't they?"

Vanessa answered with another pat on her

hand and Callie managed to stem her tears and scan the crowd still filing into the room. There were the Daltons, Taylors, Sanchezes, Brandts, and the Johns. And last, the Abernathys. Not only were they the groom's family, but also the largest in the Bronco area.

When Tyler appeared, he was flanked by a pair of brothers. Since she'd never met them formally, she wasn't exactly certain if she was attaching the correct name to each face. But she thought the man on Tyler's left was Dean and the one to his right was Garrett. As they took their seats, none of the family paused to look back at the guests sitting behind them. Therefore removing the chance of them making incidental eye contact with anyone. But what was she going to do during the reception? Turn her head and behave as though he was a stranger? Rather than the man she loved?

She pushed the painful questions aside as she watched a very young flower girl strewing petals of roses and peonies, along with an equally young boy bearing the rings on a brocade-covered pillow move slowly down the aisle. When they reached the altar, a woman with long black hair and wearing a yellow flounced dress walked up to a standing microphone and began to sing in a beautiful soprano voice. Callie blanked her mind as the lyrics about love and forever filled the room. But when the music suddenly changed to the "Wedding March," she, like everyone else in the room, turned to watch Melanie float down the aisle, escorted by Winona Cobbs.

With her blond hair fashioned in an intricate updo and her face glowing, she was a vision dressed in white lace and silk. Her bridal gown, fashioned in a mermaid style, had a deep V neckline in both the front and back. A line of tiny lace-covered buttons ran the short length of the bodice in the back and stopped just as the silk flared out at her hips. The train, which flowed from the back of her veil, was of tulle and lace and fastened to a tiara. A page boy, no older than ten and wearing a dark suit, faithfully carried the long train as Melanie and Winona made their way down the white-carpeted aisle.

Callie couldn't ever remember seeing a more beautiful bride or a wider smile than the one on Gabe's face when Winona placed Melanie's hand in his.

After the minister said a prayer, another song was sung by the soprano, and then Gabe and Melanie held hands and exchanged vows to love and honor each other for the rest of their lives.

By the time the minister prayed again and pronounced the couple husband and wife, Callie had to pull another tissue from her purse and dab her eyes.

Sniffing, she said to Vanessa, "I've never seen a lovelier wedding. Until I see yours and Jameson's, that is. But I'm sure yours and Jameson's will be just as beautiful."

Vanessa leveled a pointed look at her. "Callie, when we get to the reception, I want you to drink three glasses of champagne in rapid succession."

Callie's mouth fell open. "Do you want to carry me out of here?"

"No. I want you to relax and enjoy yourself."

Enjoy herself and forget the fact that Tyler had ended their relationship. That's what Vanessa had really been telling Callie, she thought, as a few minutes later she stood at the edge of the reception crowd and slowly sipped from a fluted champagne glass.

But all the champagne in the world couldn't push Tyler from her mind. In fact, she was beginning to think now would be a perfect time to approach him. He might rebuff her, but with this many people around, he couldn't run away completely.

After finishing the first glass of champagne, she felt relaxed enough to move around the ballroom, where at one end, elaborately decorated tables had been set up for cutting the five-tiered cake and showcasing the drinks to accompany the sweet concoction. Across a wide expanse of parquet dance floor, a six-piece band was already playing an assortment of new and old songs.

Callie was talking to Brittany and Amanda—Melanie's friends and former next-door neighbors at her Bronco Heights' apartment—when, from the corner of her eye, she spotted Tyler standing next to one of his brothers and another man she didn't know. Perhaps it was his father, she thought. He appeared to be the right age and his dark looks were similar to those of the Abernathy brothers.

If things were different, Tyler might have been escorting her around the crowd to meet his immediate family. As it was, he barely darted a glance in her direction.

While she contemplated that sad notion, Brittany's husband, Daniel, invited his wife to dance, then moments later Amanda's husband, Holt, suggested they follow the couple onto the dance floor. Callie was watching the two women leave on the arms of their spouses when someone tapped her on the back of the shoulder.

Turning, she was more than surprised to

see one of Tyler's brothers. There was a faint smile on his face.

"Ms. Sheldrick, would you care to dance?"

"Thanks, but I'm not much of a dancer."

"That's okay. I'm not, either," he said.

He reached for her hand and Callie didn't have the heart to pull away from him. But what would Tyler think?

He won't think a thing, Callie. Because he doesn't give a damn.

Ignoring the taunting voice in her head, she allowed him to lead her onto the crowded dance floor. As he curled an arm around her waist and guided her into a slow two-step, he said, "By the way, in case you don't know, I'm Dean Abernathy. Tyler's brother."

"I guessed that you were his brother," she admitted. "I just didn't know which one. Uh, how did you know my name?"

A wry twist touched his lips and Callie could only think how very much he resembled his younger brother. Tall, with the same dark hair and blue eyes.

"Tyler told me."

"Oh." What else could she say? Other than *I don't want to talk about your brother. I don't want to hear anything about him, either.* "So are you enjoying the wedding?"

He grunted with amusement. "Does any man really enjoy a wedding?"

"Gabe appears to be enjoying himself," she said crisply. "As for the rest of you men, I couldn't say."

He chuckled. "I now see why Tyler has fallen in love with you."

That brought her up short and she very nearly stumbled over his booted feet. "Pardon me?"

"It's true," he replied in a nonchalant manner. "Although, I have to admit, I was surprised by it all. What with everything he's been through. But I'm sure you know all about that. No need for me to bring it up."

There was every need, Callie thought. But she wasn't going to admit to this man that Tyler had kept her in the dark about his private life.

"Listen, Mr. Abernathy, I—"

"Call me Dean, please," he interjected.

"All right, Dean. I'll just tell you straight-out. I don't want to talk about Tyler. In fact, if I had known he was your motive for dancing with me, I never would've agreed."

He arched a brow at her. "Forgive me. I guess I got confused. I thought you cared for my brother."

"I do. I did! I mean that's all over with now," she said morosely. "Surely, Tyler has already made that clear to you. If he hasn't, I can repeat it."

"Hear me out, Callie. Tyler is in a terrible state and has been ever since he walked away from you. The only thing that will fix him is for you to go to him and let him know that you care."

She struggled to keep her jaw from dropping. "Look, we both know that Tyler has far more issues to deal with than me."

Dean shook his head. "I know my brother better than anyone in our family. And I believe you can make all those issues go away. That is, if you care enough to try."

She swallowed hard as a ball of emotion filled her throat. "All he has to do is come to me."

"True. But he's already given up a lot in his young life, Callie. He shouldn't have to give up his pride, too."

Fearing that her tears were going to resurface, she bit down on her bottom lip. "Okay, Dean. I'll try to say hello to him."

Smiling, he squeezed her hand and, with sudden surprise, Callie realized that this man didn't just want his brother to be happy, he wanted her to be happy, too.

"Would you like another drink, sir? Champagne? Punch?"

"No, thank you," Tyler told the young waiter who already looked exhausted from catering to the massive crowd. "You can take this empty glass, though."

"Certainly." The waiter placed the empty glass on the round tray he was carrying and moved on to another group of people who'd drifted away from the ballroom and into an adjoining lounge.

Tyler had no inclination to dance. Nor did he want to stand around and watch Dean waltz Callie across the room as if he owned her.

Why shouldn't your brother dance with Callie if he wants to? He's unattached and so is she. You saw to that.

Disgusted with the mocking voice in his head, Tyler changed his mind about having another drink and turned in the direction of the bar. But his intentions were suddenly halted as he found himself standing face to face with Callie.

"Hello, Tyler."

As soon as the wedding guests had begun to file into the ballroom, he'd spotted her coming through the door with Vanessa and Jameson. She'd looked so achingly beautiful; he'd wanted to go straight to her and gather her into his arms. But fears and doubts had held him back. And now he was very much afraid that he was losing the battle to keep his distance.

"Hi, Callie."

She continued to look at him with those warm brown eyes until his surroundings faded into nothing but swirling colors, the muted sounds of clanking glasses, music and laughter.

"I think we should talk," she said without preamble.

Damn it, he was shaking inside. "Not now. This isn't the time or place."

Her nostrils flared. "You really have a hang-up about time, Tyler. You need more, but more isn't enough. It's not the right time, or later would be a better time. Well, I happen to think we need to talk now."

She reached for his hand and Tyler couldn't resist as she led him through the crowd. When they finally reached a cleared area of the room, he realized they were standing near a pair of French doors that led out to a patio.

"Let's go out here," he suggested. "It'll be quieter."

She nodded in agreement and, with a hand at her back, he guided her through the door and onto an expanse of rock floor that looked out at a wooded area of evergreens and hardwoods. Two other couples were milling around the opposite end of the patio, but neither bothered to look in their direction.

Chaise lounges and armchairs made of dark polished wood and white cushions were grouped at both ends of the patio. Callie took a seat on the end of one of the lounge chairs and Tyler sat in an armchair directly across from her.

She looked at him and smiled just like she had whenever they'd made love, and his heart ached just a little more.

"It looks strange to see you without Maeve," she said.

"Mom offered to keep her today. She said a wedding wasn't the easiest of events to take a baby and I agreed."

"Oh. I thought your mother would be here to see her nephew get married."

Tyler said, "Mom was planning on coming, but right now she's hobbling around on a cane. She dropped a fifty-pound sack of feed on her foot."

Clearly puzzled, Callie asked, "What was she doing with a fifty-pound sack of feed? Isn't that a job for you men?"

He wasn't going to let her question irk him because he realized she wasn't all that informed about ranching life. Not any more than she was about the demons that had driven him from her bed two weeks ago.

"She's a ranch woman, Callie. She loves to help with the outdoor chores. Especially when things are super busy and we need extra hands. But sometimes she attempts to do things she shouldn't."

"I see. Well, I hope she gets well soon. And little Maeve—is she doing okay?"

She was making small talk while all he wanted was to snatch her up and kiss her over and over. He wanted to taste the sweetness of her lips, to let the warmth of her body melt away the icy pain inside him.

Clearing his throat, he said, "Maeve is walking now. Her steps are still a bit shaky, and she takes some spills, but she's getting the hang of it."

Her eyes grew wide. "Maeve is walking? That's wonderful! You must've been thrilled..."

Her words trailed away and Tyler was struck hard as he watched a veil of moisture build in her eyes.

"I thought about you, Callie," he said huskily. "I wanted to call you—"

Without allowing him to finish, she jumped to her feet and walked over to the edge of the patio. A carpet of perfectly manicured green grass stretched to the edge of the woods and, for a brief moment, he feared she might step off the patio and simply keep walking until she was completely out of sight and away from him.

He couldn't let that happen.

As he walked up behind her, a gentle breeze

ruffled the hem of her dress and teased the dark waves of her hair. The closer he drew to her, the more he picked up her delicate scent and, when he finally reached her, he couldn't stop his hands from resting on her bare shoulders.

Dipping his head to her ear, he spoke in a choked voice. "I've missed you so much, Callie. All I've wanted this past couple of weeks is to be with you again."

She turned to face him and Tyler didn't miss the anguish in her brown eyes.

"Then why didn't you come to me? Let me know that you hadn't put me out of your life?"

Regret pushed a groan past his tight throat. "Because I'm no good for you. Because you deserve much better than me, Callie."

Her hands came up to gently rest against his chest and Tyler wondered if she could feel his heart hammering for her and her alone.

"I should be the one to decide that, Tyler. And you didn't give me that chance. You ran out—"

To Tyler's horror, he felt tears burning the backs of his eyes and he knew with sudden certainty that he would never want to give her up, or the generous love she'd tried so hard to give him.

"I'm sorry about that, Callie. Truly sorry. I took the coward's way out because that's what I am. What I've been for a long time."

Perplexed, she shook her head. "How could you say something like that, Tyler? I can't understand this self-loathing attitude you have."

He inhaled a bracing breath. "You can't understand it without knowing the truth. And there's so much I need to tell you." With a hand on her upper arm, he led her over to one of the lounge chairs. "Let's sit here together."

Once they were seated close together on the cushion, Tyler reached for her hand and held it tightly as he summoned the courage to meet her gaze head-on and answer the questions swirling in her eyes.

"Do you mean about your marriage? And Luanne?" she asked.

He nodded and began to explain how he'd met Luanne while on a cattle-buying excursion to Cheyenne with his brothers. She'd been on her way to Jackson Hole on a skiing trip, but because of bad weather, her flight had been delayed. The attraction between them had been instant and he'd ended up flying back to Chicago with her. After two short weeks there, they'd married before either had ever really thought things through.

"Only a few months passed before our marriage was in turmoil," he told Callie. "She hated Montana and wanted us to live in Chicago. I couldn't do that. Everything I have—my work and livelihood, my family and home—is here."

"Surely, Luanne knew that before you married," Callie reasoned.

"She did. But she believed she could force me to leave it all behind. I didn't understand how much she longed to be in the city, any more than she understood that the Flying A was my lifeblood. My biggest mistake, Callie, was trying to hang on and turn a wrong into a right."

"But the two of you eventually had a daughter," Callie pointed out. "There must've been some feelings between you."

A rueful grimace tightened his features. "When Maeve arrived, we both had hopes things would get better. But Maeve cried and cried. Even when she wasn't colicky, she was cranky. I didn't know a thing about babies and when I tried to hold or pacify my daughter, she must've sensed how tense I was. She would only cry louder."

Callie placed a hand on his forearm. "You're trying to tell me you weren't the best of dads?"

"With Maeve constantly screaming and Luanne was always yelling at me, it was more than I could take. I began to stay away from the house, later and later. Just so I wouldn't have to deal with any of it."

"Hiding from the problem probably wasn't the best way to handle things, Tyler," she said. "But that hardly makes you a monster."

"Maybe not. But I'm the reason Luanne is dead. I'm alive, Callie, and she's gone. All because I couldn't be a good father or a decent husband."

Shaking her head, she scowled at him. "How could you say such a thing?"

"I came in late one night to find Maeve throwing a fit and Luanne hurling ultimatums at me. She handed over the baby, then saying she had to get away for a while, grabbed the car keys and left."

"And you're racked with guilt because in your mind you caused her to have the car accident," Callie stated knowingly.

Tyler groaned. "Guilt has been my companion for so long now, I wouldn't know how to get rid of it. And why should I try? Luanne fell asleep at the wheel. Because she'd been exhausted. Because I hadn't been there to help her deal with our daughter."

Callie wrapped her hand around his and squeezed it tightly.

Her touch was like a lifeline to him and

he wondered how he'd managed to survive without her these last two miserable weeks.

"You should try, Ty, because you deserve to be happy," she said gently. "Yes, Luanne is gone. And yes, you made mistakes with her. But you're human and, unfortunately, that's what we humans do. But that hardly means you have to punish yourself for the rest of your life."

As he studied her lovely face, he could see that she truly meant what she was saying. She didn't view him as an unfeeling monster. She simply saw him as a man who'd made mistakes. And suddenly the dark pain he'd carried inside his heart for so long began to ebb away like the ocean tide.

Wrapping his arms around her, he pulled her into his chest. "You make me so happy, Callie. I love you. Truly love you. But I'm afraid of losing you. That's why I ran the other night. I thought I could outrun my feelings, but I can't. When I saw you here at the wedding, I realized I could never let you go."

She clung to him tightly and then, easing

her head back, she smiled at him. "I think you already know how I feel about you, but I'll tell you anyway. I love you, Tyler. And I never want to let you go. We're going to be happy—together."

He kissed her forehead. Then drawing her into his arms, he covered her lips with his and tried to let his kiss convey how much he loved her. How much he would always need her in his life.

Once their lips finally parted, she lifted her fingertips to his cheek and gazed at him with love that was so warm and real it filled his heart to the very brim.

"When we first met, Tyler, somehow— deep down, I knew you were the man I'd been waiting and hoping would come into my life. Now you're truly here at my side and the joy I feel at this moment is too great to measure."

"It couldn't be any more than the joy you've given me," he murmured, then after placing another long kiss on her lips, he gently pulled her to her feet. "Come on. Let's go back to the reception. I want to introduce you to my father and brothers."

Her light laugh was full of delight. "They might get the idea that we're a couple."

Grinning, he squeezed her hand. "We are, Callie. A *real* couple. Now and always."

Later, Callie and Tyler were helping themselves to punch and wedding cake, when Winona Cobbs emerged from a group of Abernathys. Most usually, the psychic's fashion choices could only be described as outlandish, but today she was a bit more subdued in an emerald-green satin dress that billowed out from her waist. A fascinator, with the same green-colored plumes and a net that draped across her forehead, held her white hair in place.

Winona had been the perfect person to walk Melanie down the aisle, Callie thought. After all, the old woman was the very reason Melanie had moved to Bronco and, ultimately, met the love of her life.

A smug smile was on Winona's face as

she approached the couple. "Tyler, Callie, I wanted to wish you happiness with your future together."

Callie's brows shot up as she glanced at Tyler's bemused expression then back to Winona. Whether the old woman truly was a physic, Callie couldn't say. But one thing was certain, Winona had known all along that Tyler was the perfect man for Callie. Her days of wondering if a prince would ever walk into her life were over. He was now standing right by her side.

"But how did you know about—"

"The bridal shower," Winona interrupted. "I told you the signal was strong then. It was even stronger back at the Fourth of July barbecue."

Callie's jaw dropped as she stared incredulously at the old woman. "But I didn't tell you about noticing Tyler that day."

"You didn't have to, dear."

Winona winked and smiled, and headed off toward another group of wedding guests.

No doubt to spread hope to another lonely heart.

"What was that about?" Tyler asked as he slipped his arm around Callie's waist.

Her smile was impish as she looked up at him. "Oh, it's just Winona's way of spreading the love."

* * * * *

LET'S TALK

Romance

For exclusive extracts, competitions and special offers, find us online:

Or get in touch on 0844 844 1351*

For all the latest titles coming soon, visit millsandboon.co.uk/nextmonth

*Calls cost 7p per minute plus your phone company's price per minute access charge